A Kidderm

CW01659216

By

R A Zantis

ISBN: 978-1-918264-01-2

Contents

Introduction

Welcome to a feast of tales. Zantis carefully steers the reader into different worlds and times, cultures, and traditions, through fact and fiction with a lightness and ease. With well-chosen words we can visualise characters and places and forge deep connections to the heart of the story. We are sometimes left reflective, sometimes outraged, and other times intrigued and tantalised and heading for the computer for additional research. Every story has a different texture, every conversation a different rhythm, tension builds and recedes or builds and overpowers. It is a fascinating journey.

The opening story, *A Kidderminster Tale*, is set in the Midlands where an unsuspecting family find themselves under the spell of the insidious creep of an organisation which portrays itself as one big benevolent family. In the next, *A Swim in Da Nang*, we find ourselves thousands of miles away on the Vietnamese coast, taunting the boiling sea then battling for life against the tumbling undertow.

In *Runner Bean Stew*, Zantis conjures up tastes and smells of a beloved mum's kitchen with stories of food and childhood, steeping the family heritage in a 'glug of olive oil' and 'a handful of parsley.' It is a story of the profound need to honour tradition and capture it for future generations.

From contemporary life in England, we are transported to a barely post-war Greece. In the blazing white heat and dazzling blue of *Agoraki*, we enter the dark recesses of a café cave, the strong aroma of fresh coffee grounds, simmering in the 'briki' on the stove and the actors poised at the end of one conflict and on the razor's edge of another.

In *Red Herring*, the reader is invited to recline on a lounger in Coverack, Cornwall. All is contentment. We then observe an unravelling, the fractured layers of recall and intrigue, of beach, of bodies, a lacunary mind and a 'clean blow to the head.'

In *The Weight of a Bell,* we meet Luke, (it feels like Somerset), a lost boy temporarily saved from the brutal present by the toll of a bell and the 'colour, intricacy, and wealth of old things' inside the sanctuary of St. Leonard's.

In the story *Arina,* Zantis describes a woman's desperate bid to escape from domestic abuse against the glorious setting of Katastari. The picture-perfect world disguises the bleak horror of violence where a man's gift to his wife is a meat cleaver which dangles heavily and conveniently from the whitewashed kitchen wall as a reminder to the terrorised woman of what will happen to her if she leaves.

From Katastari we travel to Warsaw in *Last Stop*, to meet our 'not a proper Jew' protagonist struggling to find standing space in one of the countless cattle trucks heading to the East. Inside the claustrophobic trap, our passenger shares his thoughts, sometimes out loud, as the cattle truck rumbles to its destination.

We move from 1940's Poland to contemporary England in *The Poem*, to a chilly uninviting sea where past and present move with the sea's lap, the cold ocean and sea fret merge and the question of when flotsam becomes jetsam has an even greater significance.

In *Nancy's Video*, Zantis gently navigates the painful complexities of carefully managed end of life care. This story shows the importance of getting crucial details of life and death plans plainly shared with all the family.

The following story, *Yellow*, addresses end of life care from a very different perspective, one which shows a mind wandering with contented resignation and some animation towards its end, leaving behind a living miracle.

The penultimate story, *Jack and Kate*, is wrapped in sadness from beginning to end, tracing the everyday challenges of making and executing life changing decisions during a short car journey.

Finally, in *The Kidderminster Coffee Club (pt 1)* we meet the 'Once Were' group peopled by many, including 'Four Tops' never warm unless he wears four layers of clothing, who expound the pleasure of well-made coffee and the delight of good cake. The men chat about life changing moments and the unexpectedly positive outcome of the 'almost missed' phone call.

These stories weave together humour and pain, the importance of family and connection and will leave you wanting to read Zantis' next collection. I guarantee it.

Alex Coutts Fender (August 2025)

Alex Coutts Fender has a background in Law, Education, Celebrancy, Counselling and breeding Pedigree Whippets. Alex is a Holocaust Educator, supporting Holocaust survivors in Outreach sessions, working in Poland and moderating Lessons from Auschwitz submissions.

"Many a true word hath been said in jest."
William Shakespeare, ***King Lear***

A Kidderminster Tale

0500 Wednesday 11th December 2013

There was loud banging downstairs. Persistent and deliberate. I slipped out of bed, peeked out the Velux window of my top floor bedroom. Lights were going on in the other houses forming the small cul-de-sac.

Two police officers stood in the street, looking up. They had an unmarked police car. They spotted me.

'Can you come down?' one shouted. 'It's the police.'

I grabbed a robe.

Not just constables then? Sergeants.

One introduces himself as Sergeant King. He places a boot across the doorway. We manage a good look at one another. He is mid-thirties, fair hair, a little shorter than me, bristling with confidence. The other is similar, except he is quiet.

"Tom? Your wife has made an allegation - against you. You are under arrest on suspicion of harassment of your wife."

This ought to come as a shock, but it is not. This is everything I had warned my Inspector about months ago.

‘Please make a record of this,” I ask, knowing what might lay ahead.

King cautions me. I don’t have to say anything unless I want to. And I so do. I wait for him to finish his word-perfect delivery. Odd to my ears, hearing the caution being applied to me. At me. How many people have I cautioned in the past? Countless no doubt, being a serving police officer myself.

“Why aren’t you interviewing me voluntarily?” I say.

They seem to exchange blank looks.

“I don’t know,” says King.

I sigh.

“I need to put on some clothes,” I say.

They follow me up.

“You can search the house while I get ready,” I said, grabbing a fresh shirt.

They remain still, just their eyes follow me.

“She made an allegation I had a knife last time. Said it was under my pillow. How about you look there? Another time it was a shotgun. Why don’t you have a proper look while I’m in the bathroom?”

It clearly isn’t the plan to look for anything else. They are just tolerating me. I grab a jacket, search for my wallet, and pocket my keys. They lead me down the stairs into a chill morning air. It’s still dark. My neighbours are up at the windows, surreptitiously following my footsteps to the police car. I almost feel relieved to disappear into the back seat. I am taken to Worcester Police station, a station I know well. I am booked in and body searched. The Custody Sergeant looks extremely irritated. He is skinny, with dark curly hair. He has a rat-like visage, made more studious by horn-rimmed glasses that bridge a thin nose. Why he is so agitated, I can’t figure out.

Once the search is over, he orders another. I must have looked askance.

"Because of the danger you represent to your wife and children," he explains curtly. They had a cell ready for me. I ask for a Bible.

*

It wasn't so far back. We were a young family moving to a new home. Selling up my first house in Solihull, for a four-bedroom house on the edge of Cleobury Mortimer. The views from the front of were picture postcard, green hills, grazing sheep, plenty of trees. We were out in the countryside, but still within walking distance of a town and all its amenities. I had to pinch myself. I had given up the frenetic policing of a city to be a beat copper. I got given a community. And I would be 'the' community officer. I would have to slow down. I would be able to spend more time with my beautiful wife, Annabel, and my equally beautiful 5-year-old son Connor.

Four happy years passed, as quickly as sand through my fingers. After the birth of our second child, George, Annabel started working as a yoga instructor at a gym in the heart of Kidderminster, a commute of around 13 miles, half an hour by car.

One evening, Annabel came home, all bubbly and breathless, looking fit to burst.

"Tom, I've met a really nice couple at the gym…they run a church in Kiddie… called Possibilities…they've invited me to come along. I'd really like to go."

Annabel was raised a Catholic. She preferred a modern service to the relative austerity of traditional churches. After we wed, we found one that met both our needs in Solihull. There was a vitality about the people who went there, music came out through guitars and drums, with young people playing them, and we sang modern songs not ancient hymns. Loud and celebratory songs. I loved it, so did Annabel, up to a point. Since we moved, Annabel had yearned for the spiritual support of our church. On her mention of Possibilities, I felt genuinely happy.

The Sunday afternoon she came back from a service there, she looked miserable.

"What's up?" I said.

"I'm never going there again. They're crazy."

"What happened?"

She shook her head, like she couldn't believe what she was about to say herself.

"It were crazy. People jumping around. A bit weird. People shaking."

It was difficult for Annabel to explain everything. She made a pathetic attempt to mimic the movement of shaking people. There was something about speaking in tongues.

First, I laughed and then we both laughed. I think she felt better. After that, I forgot about it.

A few weeks went by, and Annabel arrived from work in a similar state of excitement.

"I'm going back to try out with the church," she said immediately.

"You mean Possibilities?"

"Yeah."

"But why? I mean. What's changed?"

"I really like them," she said, providing no further explanation.

Sunday came. I waited home with the boys. On this occasion when she returned, she was buzzing. Exuberant. She came home the same the following Sunday, and the one after. Her attendance became routine. She told me they ran a Sunday school for the kids that ran parallel with the service, so soon after we all went along. So I went.

The appeal was immediate. A radiance of smiles, warmth, and friendliness. Welcomes were supplied from every corner. The couple who ran Possibilities were Phil and Clare, a married couple. A very attractive couple. Slim and athletic. Phil with his shock of blonde hair, and Clare with a trendy French looking bob. Both exuded charm. My immediate impression was they received newcomers like an open door, both approachable and unconditional. The setting for Possibilities, a registered charity, was an old building located at the base of a large geographical dip, down Sexton Lane, an area of extreme beauty. Imagine a green and lush hollow, a hidden emerald, a secret garden. At one edge there were staggeringly high walls which protected an empty and ruined Victorian Mill, four and a half floors tall. Its blackened bricks were brightened with shining garlands of ivy. Two huge iron gates formed an entrance, at one time parted to allow workers to pour in, in droves, to labour at the textile factory. That was years before. Shop floors had been converted into offices and art studios, industrial machines replaced by desks. At the end of a winding corridor was a huge conference hall. Modern in décor. Square lights threw off a harsh light from a vast suspended ceiling. The entire floor was covered in dark grey heavy-duty carpet. The walls were off white. It wasn't particularly pretty, but fulfilled a purpose. In one corner, a large circular stage rose three steps higher, and chairs were set out in rows to face the stage, with a central aisle like in a church, it was perfect for conducting a religious service. The band played merry songs of worship. Phil led the services, speaking at length, about community, about what it meant to be a true Christian. He emphasised the importance of family, and described us in the room as a large family. When we emerged from such services, I felt elated. Not just me. Everyone seemed to have been affected, and left with a bounce in their step. We emptied out via a back door, where the history of the place immediately resurfaced, underlining an innate sense of spirituality. A crop of quiet buildings reached out to the left, a space of grass patches spread to the right, protected by a canopy of tall trees. An ever present but silent witness, the river Stour, quietly wound its way through this small Eden. Perfect.

*

There wasn't much I could do in my cell, so I opened the Bible at no particular page. There ought to be a passage to help get me through this moment. Maybe if I went go to any page, I would find something. I believed in God. And that there would be something.

A custody assistant came to fetch me. He led me to an interview room. The Duty Solicitor was there, waiting. He nodded for me to sit down with him.

"Hi," he said, "My name is Mike."

I told Mike about Possibilities and how it had played a role in ruining my marriage.

After a brief consultation, two new faces appeared. A plain clothes officer, 40-ish, Irish looking, I only remember his as 'the Irishman'. He had pale skin but with shiny jet-black hair. Alongside him was a younger woman detective, mid 20's smartly dressed. The Irishman held out a witness statement. He shuffled its pages before starting up the tape. Then they started on me.

The Irishman assumed a stern demeanour.

"The reason why you are here is…you have been harassing your wife," he said.

*

It began with several invitations to dinner. Phil and Clare were excellent hosts. Phil was a creative cook. A master at making fresh pasta starting with water and flour. He'd roll out the dough and knead it in front of us, deft hands moulding a shapeless blob into real pasta shapes amid smiles and jokes. Clare seemed to specialise in fine wines just right for the meal. A specific wine appropriate to a particular course of food. They were both knowledgeable. Conversation was lively and funny. Educational too. We were encouraged to better understand the distinction of quality wines and to bring something on a par with them whenever we were guests. We reciprocated by hosting back. It was an expensive undertaking which my gut told me was not sustainable. I put that sentiment to the back of my mind, trying not to think about it. Instead, I told myself, I like this new life. And Phil. What a guy! He reads The Times, he is bright, personable and light hearted. A man who embraces life and all its luxuries. Wears bright pastel shirts with white collars. It wasn't long before I started to wear similar bright shirts. I wasn't the only one. Most of the men coming to Possibilities liked to emulate him, to the point where it seemed only bright pastel shirts were in fashion.

The festive season came around. There was an official Christmas Dinner at Stone Manor House, to which a select few were invited. It felt good to be part of the few. Phil and Clare sat at the top table, enjoying the best wines. We sat at tables before them, dining from a set menu. It was a stark contrast, a clear pecking order. And the cost, monies which I discovered covered not only the bill for our food and drink, but that of Phil and his entire family. Six in all.

When the evening drew to a close, Annabel and I got into a taxi. I was beside myself, fit to explode. I couldn't help my feelings from gushing out.

"Why are we paying for Phil and his family, Annabel? It doesn't sit right with me. Does it with you?"

Annabel shifted uneasily in her seat.

"Yeah, I know," she grimaced. "You are right, but…I don't know. I think we should."

We were on a different page.

On Christmas Day we received another invitation, this time to have dinner at Phil and Clare's house.

"What do you think?" I asked Annabel. "Is it right them asking for 75 quid per couple?"

"I think it'd be really good," she said. I was confused. I had to really think about this.

It was true that neither of us wanted to miss out. It would definitely be fun. So what's 75 pounds? I didn't want Annabel to feel bad. Of course we went. Everyone who wanted to attend had to present a specific bottle of champagne. I remember seeing 20 of them being sampled by Phil and his family, while the rest of us never got a sniff of it. I think inwardly, we knew it wasn't meant for us.

A sense of resentment built up inside me, starting from the pit in my stomach. I openly expressed my concerns among other circles within Possibilities.

Some kind of pushback didn't take long, first a couple of friends within Possibilities came round to our house, a spontaneous call. First on the pretext of it being social, then changing tack and trying to persuade me about how being part of Possibilities was excellent value for money, even going as far as scolding me, telling me I was wrong to be quibbling. I wasn't persuaded and it didn't deter me from expressing to them my displeasure at how things were working out.

One day, we were at home, when Joyce, Phil's PA, turned up out of the blue. She specifically asked for me.

She wasn't happy.

"I understand you don't like paying money towards Possibilities Tom."

I was dumbfounded, not sure what to say to this, so I let her go on.

"Phil and Clare do a lot for you, Tom. You must know that."

"Ok."

She carried on speaking words and I nodded along. I can't remember all of the justifications. She was very convincing and of course she was right. I smiled. Joyce looked reassured. As soon as she realised she was winning she was smiling along with me, gaining more confidence along the way.

"If you want the best Tom," she said as her parting shot, "You have to be the best."

*

The Sunday service usually went like this. A band played, young musicians sang bright joyful songs. Phil followed this with a sermon, usually an extract from the

Bible. After that, a guy called Raymond took over, gave us updates on what was happening or soon to happen, reminding us about how much Possibilities was doing for all of us, detailing social events designed for adults and children.

"Don't forget the mindfulness sessions," he would say with a beaming smile, "Or the fitness classes...something for everyone folks...and a big cheer for all those involved in the charity work...nights for the homeless."

After the mutual cheering and satisfied looks petered out, Raymond left the congregation with a strong message.

"Ask yourself, what are you giving back?"

He stressed the issue of tithing, referencing the Bible in both the Old and New Testaments. There were between 40 and 50 people in the room, and I was aware that many were making regular payments to Possibilities via direct debits and standing orders. I was one of the few who wasn't.

I had also been informed that some had remortgaged their properties in order to meet the sums they paid in. They were willing and unbegrudging. Not like me. It was hard to work out why I was different from them. I became more disgruntled as time went by.

One day, after a service, I was ushered by Clare up to Phil's office. This was set in a separate building, directly opposite the exit to the conference hall. I followed Clare up some cast iron steps leading to Phil's office.

Phil was there waiting, seated behind a large oak desk. His face warmed as I entered. Clare peeled off to one side. Phil asked me how my family and I were doing. I told him we were good. He looked pleased. Then he got to the point.

"Tom, if you're going to be a practising Christian…"

He talked at length, reeling off benefits that my family and I were receiving. It was a good sale. I was convinced.

"This really is for *your* benefit Tom," added Clare. "I'm sure you can see that."

"How much are we talking?" I wanted to know.

"More than 10%," Clare said without hesitation.

It was impossible to argue with anything they were saying. It was all true. I felt guilty and ashamed. Life was better with Possibilties there. Shortly after the conversation in Phil's office, I committed to paying a monthly amount to the charity. It was all there in the Bible. A tithe equals 10%. Why shouldn't it be more? In the following years, I paid regular sums between £250 and £300 a month.

*

I had a feeling the two detectives had already formed an opinion. I was guilty in their eyes. It was a formality to get it rubber stamped by a court. Annabel had them convinced, and her statement was a long list about all the bad things I had supposedly done. All they needed was a confession. The contrast between what they were alleging and what I had experienced was hard to reconcile when I knew I was innocent.

The Sergeant's eyes kept switching from my wife's witness statement to me then back again. He reeled off the accusations.

"Every time your wife comes home, you are standing outside the house staring at her."

"She says on one occasion, she was in town with her friend, Lynn, both of them on pushbikes, when you started following them on foot."

"On another day, you followed her up the road when she was with your son, Tom, and she had to hide behind a car so that you couldn't see them."

"Apparently you don't go to work in uniform."

The worst of all. "You tried to run her off the road in your car, didn't you?"

"Every time she drives past where you live, you're outside working on your car."

At one point, solicitor Mike intervened.

"Sergeant," he said. "Can I just ask, who is watching whom here?"

None of it was true. Most of it was preposterous. Why would she say such awful things? Yet here I was being interviewed. It was all too much.

"Please," I said. "I need to tell you what's really going on."

The officers, despite looking pained, sat back.

I spoke about what life inside Possibilities had been like. I called it out, it was a cult. I described how seemingly harmless messages over time changed who we were. Like. Children can only play with children if they are inside Possibilities. Ask yourself, they said. Why do they need to play with anyone outside?

The Detective Sergeant looked incredulous, told me he didn't believe me.

Solicitor Mike raised a hand.

"I need to stop this interview," he said. "I would like a moment with my client."

The officers rose looked put out, but left the room to allow for a private consultation.

Mike waited until they were outside before looking at me squarely in the face.

"Tom," he said. "I just had to tell you. I know you are telling the truth."

*

There came a moment when I began to ask myself some uncomfortable questions. When was the last time I'd called my family? My mother? My brothers? It was hard to recall. Just a telephone call. Checking on my sister, who lived in the south? Or my friends of old. When we did speak, it was they who called me. Conversations were brief. There wasn't much I could tell them. *I am good thank you. Have a nice day.*

Though my family never gave up on me, that meagre type of contact inevitably ebbs away. I don't think it mattered that much. I reminded myself I had a new family. The Possibilities family.

If it wasn't for the bills I would have remained blissful in my new reality.

"We can't keep doing this. I can't – keep doing this." I kept saying to Annabel.

Whenever I raised the subject, she looked very uncomfortable.

"Why even say that? I'm not leaving Tom. I'm happy here."

Annabel was now working as a yoga instructor within Possibilities. Her status among our new family had grown rapidly. She strode the grounds of Sexton Lane with greater purpose.

We got sucked in more and more. I went with the flow. It wasn't suffering. It was great. It was easier. As long as…

As long as what? You didn't fight it. Don't fight it Tom!

One morning I woke up and went to the loo. I peered into the mirror. The man looking back at me, I didn't recognise him.

Who are you?

Answer: I don't know.

Yes you do. Don't lie.

I had to strain to see. Though I lacked the blonde hair, it was Phil.

I did a double take. Yes.

It was Phil in the mirror, no mistake, Phil gazing back at me.

I donned my yellow pastel shirt with the white collar, it was my day off. I was thinking I might spend the day at Sexton Lane. Where else was I going to go? We were now used to having our free time there. Even when I was alone, I was different to the man I was before, for example, the newspaper I read. The Sun had been usurped by The Times. Pub nights had been replaced with refined evenings with friends. Almost everything revolved around Possibilities.

Even our holidays. *Holidays should never be longer than a couple of weeks.* Someone had advised me. Life is so much better now, isn't it? Don't fight it Tom. I should have felt good. I felt terrible. The cause was clear.

A piece of me was missing. The bit that made me, Me. On top of that, my finances were in a mess.

I didn't have the trappings Phil had, my earnings as a constable were moderate in comparison, plus I was paying a monthly tithe which I knew we couldn't keep up.

More importantly, this 'loss of identity' was only apparent to me. Not even Annabel noticed. I think she preferred this new 'Phil version' of me. No one else seemed to notice either. I was still Tom the local bobby, still the man on the beat. With a lovely wife and two boys. A respected member of the community and someone earning a regular salary. A family within a much greater family. None of that explained how I wasn't sleeping well, and how I wasn't feeling well. Arguments with Annabel began to crop up more regularly, and get more heated. Sometimes at 2 or 3 in the morning.

Once I made up my mind that staying within Possiblities could ultimately cost me more than money, there was no going back. My sanity was at stake. I was mentally spiralling. Real debts don't just disappear. You can't keep turning a blind eye to them. They accrue, and you have conversations in your head, mostly in the night. My fault, nobody else's. Annabel seemed oblivious to it all, and was lukewarm to, if not resentful of my protestations. She was adamant - we - couldn't - leave.

I studied her face through one Sunday service while Phil was speaking. She was enthralled, mouth agape, swallowing every word he uttered.

When I mentioned to Annabel about visiting family, saying how I'd begun apologising to friends and family for not seeing them, she would say, "We have a family here, Tom. We don't need anyone else."

She began to spend even more of her free time with Phil and Clare.

One day I couldn't contain myself any longer. I said the word. Cult.

If looks could kill. She despised me for saying it. I could tell. So I repeated it. It still sounded right. It landed hard and I could see how alarmed she was. This was beyond her control. She hurriedly went to Phil and Clare for advice.

"You need help Tom," she said on her return.

I believed her. At least that part was true.

"Phil says that you have issues that come from that time you tried to resuscitate a baby."

That too, was true. That was something I'd never got over. Unresolved.

"You need to talk to a doctor," she said.

I booked an appointment, and went to my local GP. Annabel was meant to accompany me but she ended up being late. I faced the GP alone. We went over my symptoms, how I was being affected. Matters I hadn't shared with anyone else, and could never discuss with any of my police colleagues. Such concerns were deeply shrouded in shame and weakness.

I spoke honestly about my mental wellbeing. He asked a number of questions. He leaned back in his chair before giving me his opinion.

"As far as I can tell, there's nothing medically wrong with you, Mr Stevens. Have you considered marital guidance?"

I felt an enormous wave of relief. A lightness I hadn't experienced for a long time.

"So. Am I hearing correctly? I'm not going crazy?"

"I don't think so," he said.

I couldn't wait to tell Annabel the good news when she got there. But when I did, her face turned red and she was off at me, shouting.

"How dare he say that! He doesn't know what he's talking about!"

I was speechless.

"You need help Tom. Phil and Clare have offered weekly sessions to help you get through this. Please. For me, for the sake of our children, you should do this."

"Ok," I agreed.

"If we mean anything at all to you, you need to do this," she repeated.

"Ok, ok," I said. The heaviness around my neck was already back.

I waited and waited, but the sessions never happened.

I pointed this out to her one evening. Annabel looked back at me, accusingly.

"What do you expect? All your talk about leaving us," she said. "Phil says he can no longer trust you."

*

"I don't believe you," said the Irish detective at the end of the first interview. Then I had that further consultation with solicitor Mike, when he told me he believed me and why. He went off to speak to the officers.

In the meantime, a new member of staff had come on shift. Someone I vaguely knew. She offered me a coffee, and asked how I liked it. Just that small kindness made me feel more human again.

The detectives were almost warm in comparison in the second interview, I noticed a big change in the woman interviewer especially. Instead of firing accusations, they proceeded carefully through the remainder of Annabel's statement. This was less of an interview, and more like going through the motions, an effort to get everything containing an allegation out in the air, before being invited to comment.

"You know what?" I said when they finished. "That's possibly one of the worst statements I've ever heard."

Twelve hours after my arrest that morning, I was taken before the Custody Sergeant. Both detectives were present.

"Tom," said the Irishman, what we're going to do is bail you over Christmas with conditions."

"No, you're not," I said. "This whole charade has been about stopping me getting access to my children over Christmas, and I'm not doing it. Either you charge me now or you let me go."

The Irishman looked startled.

"Well," he said hesitantly, "We can't do that."

"Well, I'll tell you what. I won't accept any of your conditions of bail. I know that means you can keep me in custody. Well fine. You decide what you want to do. Either charge me or let me go."

I stepped back while the Irishman and the custody officer talked in whispers. Then the custody officer nodded for me to come forwards.

"We're going to release you without charge," he said. I watched closely as he scribbled something on the custody record.

The statement I have seen gives no evidence of harassment. There is no suggestion of controlling, harassing, or violent behaviour. I am aware that the person in custody was issued a PIN notice (Police Information Notice) in October, but there appears to be no documented investigation around the initial allegations at the time this PIN notice was issued. In essence, there is no evidence to support the allegation made at this time. Decision is No Further Action. Released from custody.

*

When my police 'self' took over, I seized the opportunity to search the accounts at Possibilities on the internet. At that time, all registered charities had to make their accounts available to the public on request. In 2007, a sum was paid, under the title of pastoral support, of over £50000, and a further provision paid for travelling and other expenses amounted to nearly £25000. The following year, these had risen to a combined total of nearly £104,000.

Reading these numbers made me feel sick inside. I was freely handing money to Possibilities I couldn't afford. And when I'd tried to argue the imbalance in terms of financial expectations, troops would rally to tell me the error of my ways and I'd get shot down. Well, that's how it felt. Thinking back, this should have been enough to give me the resolve to get out.

As a police officer, piling up serious debts can amount to a serious disciplinary offence. To avoid this eventuality, I took the step of downsizing our home in Cleobury Mortimer to a three bed in Marigold Lane, Kidderminster. A small cluster of houses in a cul-de-sac, where Phil and Clare also lived, along with their parents and other members of Possibilities. Annabel adored the fact that we had moved even closer to our new family circle.

I think it was the bills that kept me in touch with reality. It didn't take long for them to accrue at an alarming pace once more.

And yet, I waited, and waited, for too long. For the sake of keeping my family intact. For the sake of trying to muster the courage to say enough is enough. For the moment where I couldn't stand it any longer.

*

The moment was at 3 am. We were in the kitchen. I was trembling.

"Annabel. I'm sorry, but I'm leaving."

"You can't," she said outright.

"I can't do this anymore," I said, my voice hoarse. "I can't be the man you want me to be. I can't be the man Phil and Clare, and Joyce, Ray, and all the others expect me to be."

She looked like she didn't believe I was serious.

"Do you even love me?" I said. "Cos I no longer know who I am."

At first, she said nothing. She looked cold. Cold and calculating. Not caring. Suddenly exasperated.

"So, you're just like that, you're going to up and go, are you?"

I had assembled some things. I showed her my overnight bag.

"Maybe we can put this right. But not here. Not like this."

Annabel began sobbing, quietly. I wanted to comfort her but I couldn't bring myself to do it. It was short-lived anyway. Her tears quickly transformed into loud screams.

"You! You tell your children then!"

"What now?"

"Yes," she yelled. "You tell Connor why you're going away and never coming back. Go on! Tell him now. Tell him to his face."

I was caught by surprise. I began to cry.

"What are you waiting for? He's probably awake. You tell him. You tell him now."

I felt numb, at some point I became aware I was being physically struck, a slap to the face, a punch to my body, like she finally knew there was no going back.

Annabel's hand was digging into my arm, roughly tugging me up the stairs towards the kid's rooms. Connor was awake. Sat on the edge of his bed, crying his heart out. I knew instantly, he had heard every word. Of course he had. His mum and dad were arguing at the top of their voices, of course he knew it was not good. I sat beside him and held him tightly. I felt a pain in my chest.

Annabel watched on from the doorway.

"Well go on then!"

Connor looked at me. Looking for comfort. So small and vulnerable. Our eyes met. Tears cascaded down his cheeks.

"I will still see you son," I sniffed. "I love you. I love you and Georgie. I just need to get away for a while. That's all."

How could I make him understand?

It needed time, and right then I did not have time. Annabel was flying off in a rage.

"Get out then! You've said your piece. Get out! Get out!"

She hurried me to the kitchen. I grabbed my things. One second I was at the front door. The next I was outside. Then the door slammed. My feet felt heavy as lead. I had car keys in one hand, my bag of things in the other. I stumbled to the car and sat inside for a while. Lost in the dark and in my own daze.

What had just happened? I knew a temporary place where I could stay. I called some friends. It was terrible, I said. I went to their house. Like a zombie I was led to a room and flopped onto a strange new bed. My head wouldn't let me sleep even though my eyes couldn't stay open. It wasn't right not being at home with my family. It was deeply wrong.

What have I done? I thought. *What have I done?* I turned to prayer.

Oh God, I whispered. Let sleep come. Please let sleep come...and...and...what then?

I prayed not to wake.

A Swim in Da Nang

It is Christmas Day in Vietnam. A last afternoon at the Hyatt, Da Nang. The following day, the *Asian Adventure* party would move to Ho Chi Minh, the city that was once Saigon.

Da Nang had been three consecutive days of frustration for Amy, after the madness, and the loneliness, of Hanoi. Da Nang had promised to be a break in the sun, but there had been very little of that. A strong wind prevailed instead. Parasols had to be felled by staff. The South China Sea was at its liveliest, greyest, and all the while, red flags flapped excitedly.

Nevertheless, Amy, eternal optimist that she was, persisted with her idea to remain at the hotel while her party had booked to go out and discover a local tourist destination. Today, a trip to Hoi An, sold as a gastronomic experience, and a chance to acquire local arts and crafts.

Come with us love, a couple of voices reached out.

Thinking she was lonely. A rescue attempt, a show of disappointment as she refused. She expressed her gratitude, followed by a '*no I'm fine, really,*' while waving a book in the air as proof.

The coach left after breakfast. Amy's relief was palpable. She was free to begin her sorties to the beach. Clothed in a simple white robe and a pair of sandals bearing the Hyatt brand, a luxurious bath towel (also bearing the Hyatt brand) tucked inside a stripey beach bag, she made her way, on the hour, every hour, to check on the sea, hopeful for respite, ergo, a swimming opportunity. The water's edge was minutes away. A stroll through the hotel complex, dodging ever busy staff, bowing to some in return, a quick '*sin chao,'* a reciprocal smile, a conspiratorial nod to the happy polystyrene snowmen and the grinning reindeer, as well as that busy Santa over there, still scaling the same part of the hotel.

Her intentions were clear. And though the Vietnamese were a gentle and respectful people, it was obvious they thought she was nuts.

Her route was circuitous. Firstly, skirting the edge of an Olympic sized pool, passing through a line of pagodas, (on a usual day they offered shelter from the sun, and tables for which to dine). A hop over a low white wall, then back on oneself, around the hotel grounds via a crazy paved promenade, and eventually one arrives at a wide sandy beach. From this point she felt remote from the hotel, even with the knowledge it was so close.

The sun was starting to dip. Now or never time. *They* might be back soon, noisily congregating and refreshing in an annexe close to her room. What would she have to say for herself, and her reluctance to join them?

She stood still, facing the sea, deliberating with her toes.

That's it, she decided. *I'm going in.*

As if by some kind of miracle, 'Away in a Manger' was sounding from the restaurant. In preparation for a live performance. A tinkling piano, and real young Asian voices, interpreting a dear memory of her childhood, magically transported their way to her ear on the wind. How beautiful, how pure a manifestation through those young voices. Surely, it was a sign. The same wind that was stirring up the sea, was delivering an exclusive performance.

She waited till the singers had finished.

*

The first steps were easy. It was cold, not too cold. The sand sloped gently, the waves at first only skin deep. Thousands of small bubbles of sea foam skated across the wet sand.

Before she knew it, she was thigh deep and standing at a precipice, a ledge. The waves became more violent, shoving her, if she waited long enough, one was sure to topple her. The only way to combat this problem was to dive in, head first, reduce their power by reducing her surface area.

I won't go far, she thought, *a few strokes, that's all. Then back again.*

Splash. It was a glorious feeling, the water embraced her, her whole being, her skin. The taste of it on her tongue. Her favourite kind of swimming, eyes closed, pounding the water, cupped hands, kicking her feet for maximum speed. It wasn't hard at all.

The waves carried her up and down, as if she was riding them, but close up they were so much higher than they appeared from the beach. Her efforts on the other hand, showed progression, she was moving farther out, she counted four large breakers before the waves became less troubling. Out here, the water became calmer, she rose and fell, gently, at one with the general swell.

After swimming furiously, she trod water for a while. She was able to breathe more easily. Glancing back at the shore, she saw the palm trees flapping furiously. The sky was darkening. She had gone a tad further than she would have liked, but the tide wasn't dragging her further out, nor taking her further along the beach, factors that told her she was in control.

Ok, she thought, *time to go back.*

The currents were neither for or against her. She made quick progress towards the beach. At some point the waves became more pronounced, more challenging, she had to work harder to keep her head above water, to keep her position stable. The closer she got, the more she felt the pull of a sinister undertow. A few more strokes, and the water beneath began tugging at her, pulling her down. She pressed on, resisting the tidal forces, trying her best to keep her head up, so she could take in more air. *My, this is strong*. It was no good. In a flash, she went under, was dragged, head first, into a spin. Hands and legs flailing. Water entered her nostrils. Where was up? Where was down?

She panicked. Like someone trying to rid themselves of shackles, she flapped and kicked wildly, hands and feet. By some miracle, she hit the surface. Her mouth screamed for air. She had seconds before the next breaker, then the undertow would take her again. It did. This time the water entered her lungs. She kicked out again, coughing and gagging while under the water. It was no good. She forced a turn, heading out to sea again, re-submersing herself beneath the surface and mustering all her strength to get back to where the waters had a degree of calm. It worked. She was away from the breakers. Despite feeling giddy and nauseous, she was alive. A couple of minutes later she was treading water once more.

I'm in trouble, she thought. *I have to stay calm.*

*

At the end of an evening dinner party, while talking about dear departed friends, Neil said something.

"Amy scares me when she gets in the water. Like that time in Greece once. Cornwall another time," he told the guests. "She does things... like going too far out. Or too deep. She doesn't see the risks the way I do."

He looked her way. His face carrying a tenderness.

"I do worry about you darling."

Amy squeezed his hand. He smiled back, but there was something extra behind his eyes that didn't coincide with the smile.

"It's true", she conceded to their guests, "I'm not proud of it. I couldn't even explain to anyone why I do it. I've almost drowned twice in my life. And on both occasions, it was my fault. Mine and mine alone. And someone else had to pull me out. Believe me. Only then do you feel really God awful. When they start pumping you out, and you come around. Yuk. I don't like to think about that. The craziest thing though, before I was saved, after a few seconds of that horrible realisation that I am 'actually drowning.' I've been overcome by a feeling of peace, warmth, I dunno how to describe it, almost a homeliness, a certainty that I am safe, and there's nothing to be afraid of."

Neil interjected.

"I've made her promise not to do it when we visit the Caribbean. I doubt it'll make any difference though."

The guests laughed.

After they left, the couple went about clearing the dishes.

Neil was unusually quiet.

"I don't know what I can say to make you believe I won't do it again," she said. "All I know is that this, us, is too good to waste on a poxy swim."

He kissed her, but there was still something there, some pain, behind the way he was looking at her.

"What's the matter Neil? Is there something you are not telling me?"

"Nothing," he said. "Just tired."

The morning after, when Neil had gone to work, she discovered dried blood on his handkerchief.

Six months later she took the flight to Vietnam. Neil's ticket had not been traded in and luckily had not been sold off to another passenger. She strongly felt his presence next to her when they took off, imagined leaning into him, him squeezing her hand when she got a little scared. When she got to the hotel, she removed a photo-frame of the two together from when they were out on a date.

*

If you do it long enough, even treading water can have a draining effect. She tried to think logically. *I am calm*, she thought. *Cold, weary, but calm. But I won't survive if I stay here.*

She spotted a couple walking along the beach. They were so involved with one another they saw neither her nor her robe. This was her chance to call to them. Bizarrely, she didn't, rather wouldn't. It was doubtful her voice would carry anyway. And the humiliation of her self-inflicted predicament, three days of it, before this trip was over, would be too much to bear.

Her next serious thought was: *I've had a good life. Actually. I have.*

Third thought. *I've got one shot at this. Best make it count.*

Fourth. *How am I gonna do this?*

OK. When I start to feel that undertow, I am going to swim the way I came out. Head down, like a submarine. Take a deep breath before I go, but then, don't try to come up, don't try to fight the undertow, don't worry about breathing. If I do any of those things, the sea will win. And if it does, I know what this feels like already.

She paddled her hands to orient herself towards shore, and began her approach.

"Neil?" she called out.

"Hell for leather, darling. Hell for leather."

*

The *Asian Adventure* coach was parked out front. There was a loud commotion in the lobby. A young maid was in distress, crying; a bellboy offered to comfort her. The holiday makers quickly grabbed their drinks and started cross talking, ideas and theories abounded, all related to the woman who hadn't wanted to go to Hoi An. *How old d'you think, 40? At least. No, younger, but sad, I thought sad when I saw her at Heathrow. I can always spot trouble. Travelling alone? Maybe she suffered from depression. Yes, but don't they have lifeguards on the beach 24/7? I mean, they should.* The tour rep, of a similar age to Amy, was bombarded with questions. All she could tell them so far was, there was a doctor on hand and they were waiting for an ambulance. As soon as she could, she escaped with the hotel manager behind an office door, on a promise to return with more information as soon as she had some.

*

Dr Nguyen, who spoke very good English, shook his head, put down his stethoscope, and stared stiffly at Amy. And then, he smiled.

"Why?" he asked.

"I don't know," she said softly, hands on her knees, like a naughty child.

"You don't know?"

"No."

"Did you want to die?"

"No. No. Quite the opposite. If I had felt like that, I wouldn't be here otherwise."

"And that is why you went in the water when it is at its most dangerous?"

"No. I mean, yes, well, maybe."

"Oh, I see. Maybe. Well, in that case, maybe you need a different doctor to me."

Amy relaxed, laughed. Dr Nguyen laughed too. The tension gone, they both laughed some more.

Outside the examination room, the tour rep and hotel manager gave each other quizzical looks, for all they could hear was unrestrained laughter.

Runner Bean Stew

Mum was happiest when toiling in the kitchen, knowing she was soon to have family or other invited guests around the table. Even when her health declined and she became breathless, her hands arthritic, her back a daily challenge, she battled on in with her pots and pans, continuing to play host. I loved her food, on the whole. Her Greek repertoire was better than her English, subject to a few notable exceptions. I think in all families, some recipes are often more cherished than others, variations might be loved or hated, feared even, turning on the choice of what plays the central ingredient.

For example, her avgolemono soup (literally Greek for egg lemon soup). This could be based on fish, or chicken. The fish, tossed into a pan of boiling water with all the skin and bones, fins, tail and head, surrounded with potatoes, carrots, onions and celery, finished off with a whisked egg and lemon mix that had to be blended in slowly and carefully so that the egg didn't curdle. I don't remember that version being suggested by anyone other than mum. As kids we were always hungry, so when we got this version, we quietly accepted our bowls, exchanged looks of horror before taking pains to remove the head, eyes gazing back at us from the plate, bones and the fish scales, placing the individual components of the carcass on a side-plate, an effort to salvage what we could. Mother on the other hand, would retrieve the discarded items, scoff the eyes then make a loud show of sucking out the brains, before our very eyes, then turn to face us with the expression of a cat that had just got the cream.

Without words she seemed to be saying, if you want to be clever, this is what you need to do. I remember thinking. Nope. This is too high a price mamma.

On good days she prepared avgolemono with chicken and rice in place of the fish and carrots etc. This could cause a stampede to the table. A mouth-watering aroma of the chicken version would permeate the house, highly recommending itself. My sister, 10 years ahead of me, and my brother, one year behind, might be distributed in various parts of the house, busily engaged in our own worlds, but somehow arrive at the table at almost the same time. The soup vanished quickly, lots of slurping amidst mum's chitter chatter, while we performed an unspoken competition in the knowledge that seconds were available.

Other treasured repasts included butter bean soup, infinite combinations of vegetable stew, green lentil stew, all manner of roast meats, lemony roast potatoes in garlic, stuffed peppers and tomatoes, spinach and rice pilaf, Greek salad with crusty bread, and more. Later in life, I did warm to a variation of the fish soup, some kind of nostalgic journey, but back then I drew a line at pigs' trotters, I still do today.

It sounds contradictory, we were poor back then. Mum had two cleaning jobs, dad was loose with money. Rent was permanently in arrears, the house was cold, except for in the living room where there was a coal fire. In the mornings our bedroom was more like an icebox, and before getting dressed for school we warmed our clothes on a two bar electric heater.

Being hard up meant there were tricks and routines to be mastered. For example, hiding the magnet mum stuck to the electricity meter, whilst delay tactics took place at the front door before allowing the electric man in. Cowering below the window so we couldn't be seen by debt collectors. When mum was short of an ingredient, we were often despatched next door to borrow something.

The fact that we'd eat most things, and mum was inventive, we never felt deprived. Apart from dad, who preferred to sit with his plate on a tray in front of the telly, we would sit together at the kitchen table, and mum would tell unsolicited stories, stories we'd heard a hundred times, mostly springing from her youth in a foreign land. We munched along to recollections of our ancestors, posing the odd question. Who was still alive, who was not? Sis's curiosity stirred when mum talked about romantic escapades and love affairs, ours when she spoke about guns, the effects of poverty and war. Stories about what it was really like to be poor.

I swear mum got old overnight. It hit me. We no longer had all the time in the world. What would it mean? I couldn't replicate many of her recipes, despite having written them down. Neither could sis. My brother didn't really cook. Not for want of trying. Why? Why didn't they come out the same? Years went by. Mum became forgetful. Then. One evening, sis called me.

'I thought you ought to know, mum rang to ask how to make spanakorizo.' (Spinach rice)

'But she makes it all the time,' I said.

'That's why I'm telling you now,' she said.

This was a warning on two levels. Her mind was slipping away. One. Two. No one cooked this stuff as well as mum.

Why was it such a mystery? She had a tiny kitchen, with an old gas cooker, while we had modern ones. Her tin pots, casserole dishes and frying pans, all bashed, had lost their sheen yonks ago. She had a cutting board she wouldn't part with, heavily scarred with a flaking picture of an aubergine on the reverse side. Cutlery had been collected over decades to the point where none of it matched. The refrigerator was noisy and food fell out of the small freezer compartment every time it was opened.

How did she do it? What kind of magic was involved? The one particular dish, I couldn't get close to. Runner bean stew. It sounded simple, easy to put together, a peasant dish yet it made you feel like royalty. A crusty baguette was essential to mop up that rich tomato sauce, with lots of black pepper on the side to keep it spicy.

The list of ingredients is short.

A glug of olive oil.

Half a cup of tomato puree.

Lots of runner beans, spliced with their stringy sides removed.

Onions.

Potatoes.

Carrots.

A handful of parsley.

Salt and pepper to taste.

Water.

That's it. Sounds simple right? Nope!

*

One day I went over to her house with a shopping bag and an ipad. We sat down in the kitchen.

'Mum,' I said. 'Please can we do your runner bean stew today? Also, I need to video you making it if that's ok?'

At this time, mum was in her late 80s, about 4 feet 2 inches tall. Almost everything she wore by then was a shade of purple, even her hair. I emptied the contents of the shopping bag onto the table and she smiled.

'Ok son.'

She began to assemble the correct pan and utensils that would be used.

We went slowly, step by step. Explanation videoed before prepping the relevant ingredients. Next explanation videoed before carrying out the next step. And I learned something.

A glug of oil? More like half a cup.

Onions not coarsely chopped, but ever so finely. Parsley the same. Not just thrown in any old way. It had to be an even mix. Lots of chatting about family in between, waiting for the onion to become translucent. This was how it had always been done. In the meantime, painstakingly removing the string from the runner beans with a potato peeler, cutting them in half, and slicing them down the middle. She looked at me. She was emotional.

'This is how my mum used to make it.'

I was one year old when my grandmother passed away, I only knew her through photographs, but now I know a little more through her cooking. By peeling the potatoes and cutting them to just the right size.

Remember son. Carrots have to remain chunky. Tomato puree has to be mixed into boiling water before joining the pan. The water can only barely cover the vegetables.

The salt.

Really mum? That much salt?

An unhealthy amount.

More!

A resolved look. So. Evidently yes.

Half an hour later we had a perfect runner bean stew. The potatoes have to melt a bit and thicken the sauce. Too much water and the sauce is too thin. Too little water and it goes dry.

*

It is five years since my mum went away.

I am sat with Sebastian, one of my nephews, in a tapas bar in Bromsgrove, somewhere in the Midlands. He is a bright fellow, 29, house owner, a lovely girlfriend, Zoe, who lives with him. He is also a reader, a lover of food, and a qualified engineer like me.

We tuck into patatas bravas, slow roasted pork belly marinated in apple juice, vodka prawns, toasted pita with hummus, harissa chicken. The chicken has not been properly marinated with the harissa sauce. Other than that, everything is delicious.

'Seb. Do you remember I used to tell you stories when you were young? How I used to incorporate you, your brother and sister, into those stories?'

He doesn't hesitate.

'Of course,' he says.

'And do you remember your pseudonym back then?'

'Matoto,' he says in a flash.

I can see he still owns the name and I smile. I register a warmth inside.

During my first summer in the Midlands nearly three years ago, after leaving my home county of Essex, we threw a barbeque for my brother-in-law's birthday.

I planned for lots of meats as one would expect, large bowls of traditional Greek salad and plates full of pita bread to enable guests to put together their own souvlakis. But in true Greek tradition, it never seemed enough. So, I threw in a hot butter bean soup, thinking, it is the middle of summer, we are experiencing a drought, so perhaps it won't be necessary. But what if it's cold? It turned out to be a lovely and hot summer day. A warm balmy evening. I'd prepared a huge pan of butter bean soup which I left on the cooker. To my surprise it was the showstopper, guests came up to me and asked for the recipe, some asked for more after it had gone. I could have made double and it would have been gobbled up. Maybe one day someone will record me making it in the kitchen.

I count myself fortunate to have experienced these hand-me downs, both the recipes and the stories, which to me are complimentary, far more effective when working together.

They preserve not only my mother's voice, but of the generations of women before her. Nurturing and expressing their love through food, even when they are long gone.

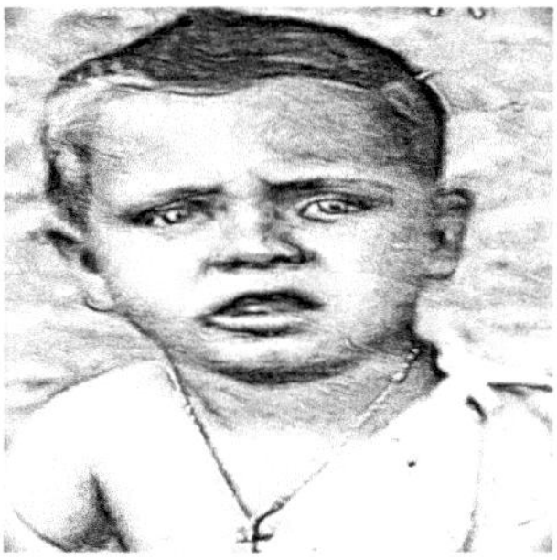

Agoraki (Little Boy)

Peter Redmond opened his eyes to find a girl in his bed, their skins glued by sweat. Her olive tone skin to his pale freckled white. Pure Med meets Brum! He chuckled to himself. He takes time to take in this beautiful contrast, marvel at his luck, then glanced at his watch on the table. He sighed. He would like to see her again, but for now there is work to do.

He taps her lightly on the shoulder, and whispers.

"Hey, Fiona, hey."

She is dead to the world. In any case, she can't go with him, but it's ok for her to stay a little longer. With regret he hauls himself from bed, then in quick succession, showers, gets dressed, and picks up a map. With the keys for the jeep in his hand he takes one more look lustful look at the girl. Her face is buried in the pillow but he can easily visualise the beauty of it from the night before. Despite her young years, she had an intensity coupled with a wicked sense of humour. From one trouser pocket he finds a wad of Greek money, and counts out due renumeration onto a side table. So much for her services, this much for a taxi home, and lastly, should she so choose, that much for a day of liberty from other men. He departs.

It is late morning, navigating out of the port of Piraeus is difficult, haulage and public transport being the main bugbear, the landscape is war torn, treacherous, and the road map bears little relation to what lies before him. Redmond decides to head in a general direction and hope that somehow, he'll see a sign or something along the way. One of the chief problems he was warned about, are the detours. The warnings come true. A broken down lorry, then an accident involving a car and a bus, then someone tells him of a giant split in the road. With the jeep he can sometimes go around. The road leading up to Vathi is more arduous. A town located higher than the Acropolis. Poor roads and rocky terrain render it naturally hard to reach. The engine struggles to manage the climb in first gear, groaning up steep, bumpy untarmacked tracks. Precarious winding roads shaped like sidewinders that do go on forever, but eventually level out on a plateau on the farthest edge of Athens. The vista behind, looking towards Athens, is breathtaking, while the view ahead opens out to what he sees is a typical slice of Greece, clusters of flat white houses blotted with blue windows and doors. A sleepy little town. Pretty despite the rubble. One day tourists will be drawn here. Hopefully by then, walls scarred with bullet holes will be gone. They will see the real Vathi, pavements lined with trees, oranges, olives, planted in a way they can hold hands, providing continuous canopies of shade for pedestrians. It is midday. Shopkeepers drop their shutters. Schools lie silent. Goats ogle from house windows, while feral cats and dogs enjoy the freedom of the streets.

He checks the time. There will be a wait. The heat will rise. Already he feels weary.

It feels like the sun is pouring molten heat from directly above, sapping the energy of whatever moves. Only flies seem exempt from this, relentlessly pestering other living creatures. The earth cracks and shimmers.

In a small central square, Redmond finds a place to park up. Next to a cluster of empty tables spread beneath the shade of a large oak tree. Finds relief there. He cannot identify the tree but it drops a scent reminiscent of the previous night. He closes his eyes, listening to the rhythm of the cicadas.

At 1 o'clock as predicted, from somewhere afar, a trumpet plays. A slow discernible lament, like cautious steps. One, two, then, gathering pace. Notes, deliberate and patient, like a funeral march, mourning the state of a divided nation.

Presently dogs begin to bark, sporadic at first, then together, though never quite in concert, chickens add vocals to the rising cacophony.

This is exactly how the old man at the port had jokingly described it to him.

"Hah. That trumpet! Not for the living. People curse, sleepers awaken, mothers mourn aloud, fathers cry through their madness, lovers release their lustful moans, everyone under the cover of the rising crescendo. Only cicadas stop their chittering," he said, "I don't know why."

The old man was laughing one minute, then feeling morose the next.

"Ach. Foreigner. That melancholy. What melancholy. You know? No. You don't. I shall explain. It affects people in different ways. It can be hope coupled with regret, or sadness and regret. But what melancholy mother Mary. And if not. What tension and dread. You know dread?"

"I know dread old man," said Redmond. "Of what? The man laughs again."

'You speak good Greek. So, I shall say. Exetatai', the old man exclaims. 'Exetatai. You know the word 'exetatai'?

"Yes. It depends."

"Why yes! That's right foreigner. It depends. In Greece, everything depends on either what you did, or which side of the fence you're on."

The trumpet blows. Right on cue. It's not so easy. Following the sound. Notes bounce off walls, first this way, then that, almost teasing the listener.

I feel stupid, he thought. *If I don't locate the source before the last notes, then I probably won't find it at all.*

But the cacophony delivers confusion, which then dwindles into nothing.

Redmond curses. If he returns to Scaramanga base empty handed, the warrant officer will be pissed. The warrant officer will take pleasure in relaying the bad news to Captain Woodward. Woodward will go hopping mad. Remonstrations will follow, just for show. Cap distrusts civilians. Failure provides evidence of Redmond's limitations, justifies the argument that the task should originally have been delegated to a military officer. And that will directly impact on the freedom he currently enjoys.

He stops in his tracks. The Agoraki can't be far. It was louder before it stopped. A few yards away, he spots a small dark boy sat on a step, staring back with similar intensity. The boy wears rags and looks hungry. A street urchin.

"To Agoraki?" He says to the boy. The boy stares, tilts his head, bites his upper lip.

Redmond produces a small coin from his trouser pocket. Holds it forward.

"Look here. Maybe a lollipop or some chocolate*,"* he says.

The boy warily approaches Redmond, eyeing the money, getting close enough to make a grab, but Redmond quickly closes his fist around the coin.

"To Agoraki," he repeats, "You know," (Redmond tries to imitate a trumpet*)* brr brr brr brr brr."

The boy frowns and points to the end of the lane.

'To prasino café Kirie," says the boy. The green café.

The urchin's eyes never leave Redmond's hand. Redmond relaxes his fingers and the coin is gone before the stranger can change his mind. Everywhere there is hunger, but today the boy will feel rich.

The green café is around a corner. He finds himself in a part of town that has seen better days. Small decrepit bungalows fronted by tall crumbling walls containing small front yards. And squeezed between such walls, what looks like a run-down warehouse.

A small cave made of concrete, it's actually a short stay café.

Outside. Two high tables, each accompanied with two chairs. Everything wooden treated with olive green paint, but not for a long time. The serving part of the café is a narrow frontage, almost pitch dark inside. The café has a single green door, tall, about five feet wide. The door is opened to rest at right angles to the building, cutting off the pavement on one side, providing a measure of shade for the tables. Inside, the entrance provides two feet of leg space before meeting a chest high counter, and a small gap on one side for people to pass in and out. Redmond stands over the counter, looking in, waiting for his eyes to adjust. A musky aroma of Greek coffee and cigar smoke combined emanate from the green darkness. A male figure sits there, his back pushing against the back wall, long legs propped up by a stool. A trumpet on his lap.

"Welcome English", says the man. "You made it. Bravo."

"I am Redmond sir. You were expecting me, Mr Agoraki?"

"You know what agoraki means?"

"Yes. It means little boy?"

"Ah. Yes. Bravo Redmond. We speak Greek then? Or English?"

"English please. I'm not so good when the Greeks get going."

The man laughed.

"But you must call me Yiannis please. As you can see, I have outgrown that name for a while now."

Mr Agoraki, Yiannis, is nothing like Redmond had predicted in his mind. Perhaps a man with a scarred face, a terrifying dwarf even. All preparatory questions to intelligence officers as to why a grown man would be widely known as 'Little Boy' were never met with a satisfactory response. Redmond now suspects, the military were either reluctant to give out false information or, and more likely, unwilling to admit they just didn't have a clue.

Yiannis is in his mid-30s, smells and looks fresh, comfortably at ease in a white collared shirt, unbuttoned at the top with the sleeves rolled up, loose fitting grey cotton trousers that look made for a suit, finished off with black polished shoes. He has a handsome face, long, clean shaven, tanned. A cigar permanently wedged between his lips. Thick brush of dark hair showing grey around the ears. He wears rectangular black framed spectacles. Had Redmond bumped into this man on the street, his first guess would be a bank manager.

Yiannis rises and begins adeptly preparing fresh coffee grounds, spooning them carefully into a 'briki' on the stove, a wide aluminium coffee pot, then guarding over it silently, stirring occasionally, waiting for it to froth. When it hisses, he pours thick dark liquid into two cups, emerges from the darkness with the cups and places them onto one of the outside tables. He goes back in, and brings out two glasses of water before signalling Redmond to sit down.

"Sugar?"

"No. Thank you."

"Good. We don't have."

Yiannis waits for Redmond to take the first sip.

Redmond raises his cup.

"Yia mas."

"Yes. To Greece."

They enjoy the coffee for some moments. Redmond knows he is being scrutinized.

"Tell me what I need to know about you English."

Redmond looks up and down the street.

"Don't worry", says Yiannis. "There is no other talking or listening here. This I guarantee."

Redmond replays his briefing from Woodward.

"Firstly. You should know this. I am not a soldier. I am a civilian and I work at the Scaramanga base for the British Army. I am here on behalf of Captain Woodward, though for that part..."

"So, you are new to this. Then why did you come?" Yiannis interrupts.

"Captain Woodward sent me. They thought…"

"No. You misunderstand. Why did **you** come to Greece?"

"Oh. Well mainly…to help with transport. It's my area of expertise, I …"

"You came here when?"

"Shortly after the regiment set up camp. In Scaramanga port. Er, about 2 months ago. In the place where I come from, the government asked for volunteers with certain skills. I got tasked with helping the Greek government establish public transport infrastructure, in other words…"

"Yes. Yes. That's all very fine. So where do you live in England?"

"Er. Is that important?"

"Oh yes. Please. Indulge. Where?"

"I was born in a small town. Kidderminster, er, I doubt you'll have heard of it, it used to be important but not so much now. It's still famous for carpets though."

Yiannis looks puzzled.

"Kidderminster is close to Birmingham? No? Well, how about…two hours from London?"

"Yes. Ok. Married? Children?"

"No. No. None of that. Not yet anyway."

"I see. Why? How old are you?"

"I'll be twenty-five next month."

"Old enough then. But. Good. Good. You like the girl?"

"Excuse me. The girl?"

"Yes. To koritisi in Pireaus. You like the girl in your bed?"

"Er. Yes. You mean Fiona? She is very beautiful, but how…"

"Please say her name correctly. She is Fionoula. She will stay at your place for a while, OK? Until this is done. Think of her as your insurance, and our continuity."

"Mr Agoraki, with due respect, what you just call my place I just rented for a couple of days. I'm guessing you already know that though. Furthermore, I wouldn't be allowed to take her back to the base, the base commander would have kittens, more than likely send me back to Britain, which would defeat…"

Yiannis threw back his head and waved a hand in Redmond's face.

"Tch. Of course you will not take her to the base, you will both stay at your place in Piraeus. Spiridoula the landlady will spit at you but she will let you stay as long as necessary. For free. You will look after Fionoula there. She will look after you. Fall in love if you can. Or at least, pretend you are serious. Be seen in public. Buy her flowers. She will pretend also, and sometimes she will tell you things, and you will tell her things. Things we need to know. So. You won't have to come here all the time. This would be very dangerous, for our organisation, for you. For the girl. It is important you understand you are already not safe. But if you do as I instruct, it will be much better. Ok?"

Redmond looked squarely at Yiannis. He wasn't joking.

"I understand. Yes. Very well."

"When you return. You can tell Captain Woodward, that Mr Agoraki, Yiannis, likes you. But Yiannis also told you, we need the weapons. Speed is critical. Things will happen, how you say, like a wildfire, as fast as fire goes dry land, and this land is cinder dry, understand?

"I think so."

"...and when it starts, it will happen very fast. Many will die on both sides, but we believe. Despite everything, we believe, God is on our side. Churchill made a promise to the Greek people. He loves Greek people, did you know that? Churchill said Greeks don't fight like heroes, heroes fight like Greeks. Your Woodward must tell Churchill that things will get very bad for us again. Communism will spread like disease. More killing, more starvation. As if there hasn't been enough. For now, communist factions are much better organised than our freedom groups. Stalin will provide for them despite his thin promises. Tell him that."

"I shall."

"And tell him the buses and the trucks, we need, but the accessories I tell you about, those we need the most. The accessories are the most important request."

"Yes."

"Yes, the accessories. Guns, ammunition. Not cheap and unreliable. The best we want. They are detailed here. Read this, memorise, burn it if you are compromised, don't trust anyone you meet along the way, but if you memorise before you return to Pireaus, that would be better. Tell your captain this is our minimum requirement. Minimum! He will say it is too much but I will say it is not enough. If he is a good captain, he will know I'm right."

Yiannis hands Redmond a note, then makes to rise from the table.

"Ok. You can go now. I like you Redmond. Truly."

"Er. Peter, please. Thank you. It was good to meet you too Mr Agoraki."

"And I am Yiannis. One more thing, you know Sintagma Square?"

"Of course, we all go there at some point, the place of the Royal Palace?"

"Yes. Ask your superiors about the great library, a rug running the entire length of the quiet rooms, commissioned by our George the first. You might recognise. From your hometown, it is possible, I believe."

Yiannis winks. They shake hands.

"I will. I shall certainly ask about that. Thank you Yiannis. Thank you for the coffee. It wasn't so bad without sugar. Do you mind telling me, why you play the trumpet exactly at the time that you do?"

Yiannis holds the back of his chair, and leans over it, closer to Redmond.

"Peter. Peter. Tell me. Where do you see the young people here?"

"Sorry?"

"Yes. Where do you see any young people in this town?"

"I…er, I don't know. I imagined they are out working somewhere?"

"Before you leave, drive to the north exit of the town, so you are heading further up the mountain. Yes? You will find it. There is a large rock at the entrance to a small olive grove. You will find your answer there."

*

Feeling vindicated, and on the way back from a successful rendevous, Redmond can't help a wide grin crossing his face. In the spirit of a foreign agent, he has memorised the note and burned it. It is late afternoon when he arrives in the suburb of Koridalos. He parks up outside the rental, and finds the 80 year old 'yiayia' sat alone at the base of the stairs to his room, like an old sentry. She is dressed entirely in black, topped with a black headscarf.

"Kali mera Spiridoula,," he says politely.

"A sto dialo", scowls the yiayia.

Redmond grins and carefully side-steps past her to go up the steps.

To his dismay, the girl has left. Someone has tidied up the room. On a table he finds a note.

'Dear Mr Redmond, thank you for the romantic proposal. I will see you in a short while. F x'

He goes over the note with a mix of pleasure and wonderment, still unsure of the relationship between Fionoula and Yiannis, but excited about the new arrangements. Captain Woodward will have mixed feelings about the outcome too, no doubt. Redmond decides he can wait, at least until he has freshened up. Another shower is required. He is emerges from the shower with just a towel around his midriff, when the girl reappears at the door. She has on a bright blue dress and flat shoes. Her hair is tied in a bun. Her lipstick removed. She has gone somewhere, and dressed down from the night they met. This is her when she is not a working girl. But she is the same girl. At least he hopes so. He smiles. She smiles back.

"You have a key it seems."

"Haven't you heard the latest? It seems I live here now. Do you mind?"

"Mind? No. Not at all. You?"

She approaches him, tracing a finger across the top of the towel.

"No. I like. But it can only be business, we can pretend to have fun in between, I think. You?"

"Yes. I like, Fionoula. I'm sure the old lady downstairs disapproves though."

"Probably." Fionoula suddenly looks sad. "And my brothers definitely the same."

"I am guessing that you are from Vathi, am I right?"

"Yes."

"I'm sorry for what happened there. Truly. It must have been awful."

She sighs, looks down, studies the floor.

"Ok. It's sad."

"It's very sad. Mr Agoraki, I mean Yiannis, told me to take a look so I went to the rock. You lost so many."

"Yes, Redmond. But you have to promise me never to talk about this though."

"I understand. And I won't. I should tell you though. Mr Agoraki told me he likes me."

"What?"

"You know. Mr Agoraki, the trumpet man."

She laughs heartily.

"What is it? Why are you laughing?"

"Oh my God. You're funny. You met a man with a trumpet. That's all. Do you know how many Mr Agorakis we have in Greece right now? You will meet many more. Maybe."

"Oh, says Redmond, laughing at himself. "Don't I feel stupid now? You need to understand, I'm new to this stuff...Fionoula."

"Come here Redmond."

She gently clasps his right hand in hers, places his palm across the side of her face, then draws it down towards her breast.

"Don't worry yourself too much," she says. "Fionoula will help."

Red Herring

The Police Sergeant assigned to my case told me he can read my thoughts, which is how he knows I'm lying. He doesn't seem to realise I can hear his though, without any magic. Truro is a small police station, not properly designed for keeping secrets. While a young officer took my fingerprints, I could hear the Sergeant talking to someone in the custody suite, clearly a man of higher rank.

"What have you got?" that man said.

"I can tell you she's a compulsive liar sir. None of her story rings true. Trouble is I think she's convinced herself otherwise, and when a woman does that you know…well, in any event, it's all over the place."

The Sergeant was huffing and puffing. Yes, I could hear that too.

"Trust me sir. Just give me a day or two, and I'll have it cracked."

"No brief?"

"No sir. But don't be fooled. As I say, she's one of those that's convinced herself she's innocent. This will take time."

"And what have we got that's concrete yet?"

"We have a body. Head injury. She was with the deceased at the material time, possibly witnesses but can't confirm yet. Other than that. She thinks she's better than us, she has money and looks, but I sense a cold-hearted bitch…"

The officer taking my prints blushed.

In the interview room, the officer assigned to my case identified himself as Detective Sergeant Gerry Anderson. He never said anything about being someone who jumped to conclusions, the alcohol on his breath, the way he looked at me, his eyes lingering over my breasts. He didn't say anything about that.

"For the tape, I am Ds Anderson. You are Patricia Coleman. Let me remind you, you're under caution. You stated earlier you had a lac-un-ary memory. I had to look that one up.

I'm going to say for the record what I think. I think it's more a selective one. What do you say to that?

I didn't say anything.

"How about we go through your story again? Take your time. Don't leave out any detail."

"Well, alright. But can't you just listen to the tape again?"

"Again," he insisted. "Indulge me."

"Well the day started with me and my husband lazing about the conservatory of the house I told you about. The cottage is called Suntrapped."

Anderson shuffled papers while I spoke. Most distracting.

"Suntrapped. That's the rented property in Coverack?"

"Yes."

"Rented at two thousand pounds per week?"

"Yes."

"And." Anderson made notes. "Who paid for that?"

"Jointly I think."

"Joint...ly. Go on then."

"Oh. Well, I was sat upright with a book in my hand. David seemed to be fast asleep; I had his head on my lap."

In my mind I pictured the rest of David's long figure stretched well beyond the full length of the sofa, his two naked feet dangling over the armrest. Not nice feet, not terrible either, and I had got used to them. I hovered on whether I should say how I felt about his feet. Not wishing to incriminate myself further.

"Go on."

"I was lamenting the late frost to him. The state of the camelias. Their brief life. Yesterday they opened their eyes for the first time, beautiful pink blossoms, ready to appreciate the world around them, you know, enjoy the coastal sunshine, and already they were tinted with brown edges."

"A frosty morning then. You said your husband woke up."

"Yes, I remember his exact words. He said. This is marvellous, isn't it darling?"

I visualised my husband's eyes open wide. The sea in them. A blue topaz, matched by a cove I used to frequent in the north of Zante. Eyes I used to trust, nestled behind pale eyelids and strawberry lashes.

"When I looked, I noticed that David was studying me. He said, Are you alright?"

"Yes. Good thanks."

"I mean – literally?"

"To be honest officer, I was irritated. You're denting my thighs, I told him. I can't feel my legs."

"Sorry darling."

"Why don't you go and make a cup of tea or something. Do something useful.

My husband made a long, showy, yawn, you know the kind you don't believe? Just before propping himself up, stretching to the ceiling. He said, I know, how about we go to the beach instead? I'll treat you to a coffee at The Shack. He made me lose track of my book.

I pointed to my book.

'Please Pattie, darling, that was his way, it is my holiday too.'

So you see officer? It wasn't even my idea.

As I said before. Then we got ready, and thirty minutes later, we were out.

David knows me. As soon as someone says the word beach, I'm halfway there. Like I see it. Hear it. Almost like its whispering to me, and me alone. I know Coverack well, its beach, scattered rocks and rockpools."

"So did you have an argument about going down to the beach?"

"On the contrary. I love the sea. I couldn't wait to feel the salty ice water shifting around my feet. Sand washing away from my toes, that feeling of falling, the touch of a great living, breathing thing.

Of course, I agreed to go with him, it was his holiday too, after all."

"Do you always talk like this?"

"I'm sorry? Like what? You said you wanted details."

"Never mind. Talk me through your journey down to the bay."

"Well, we donned our wellies, locked up our temporary home. Put the key in the key safe. Took the steep craggy path that gets us there in the quickest time. I was happy. Just the glimpses of the blueness between the bilberry, downy birch, common juniper, spurge laurel, and rowans was enough. I high fived as many leaves and berries on the way down as I could. To answer your earlier question, I can't remember if we saw anyone on the way. I don't remember if we did. The locals would know better than us anyway. It's a muddy track, even with our boots we had to keep to the drier grass, mostly on the sides, when it's there. The shade was preserving some frost on the foliage and on the grass, so it was very slippery still."

"You didn't see anyone. You're sure?"

"I can't be 100% but no."

"Right."

"Then we emerge from the wood, slow as we go past a small shared allotment with a panoramic view of the bay, take a little time to admire the flowers as we pass a long line of terraced cottages, you know those ones with pastel colours, past the social club, then onto that road which winds down steeply towards the bay.

David held my hand, most of the way. I'll admit, when we got to the café, I did forcefully tug him past it. You see, with me it is. Sea first, coffee later. It is the opposite with him.

I remember the breeze. Urging us along. Skimming the breakers. The water was half out, but I could taste the salt already. We used that old sea wall with the sea-weedy slope to get down to the beach. First, I scanned the horizons, nothing nefarious, I like to know who I'm sharing the beach with. Most of the boats were lying on their side, waiting for the tide to return. I did see four cold water swimmers gathered in bright coloured dry robes at the far end of the bay.

You said before we stopped for coffee first. Who told you that? I have no recollection. That could be a red herring. I told you, didn't I? My father was a senior detective in the Met, retired now of course, but he told me things about his investigations, about the red herrings. Every case has one, or more, he said. Don't you ever get that? He used to tell me stories about his cases. Someone will swear they saw the victim walking about a shopping centre 3 days after they were stabbed to death.

"Not really no."

"No. No. That's not how I remember it. Is it at all possible that David stopped for coffee in spite of me, and I went on alone? Yes. That's not how I remember it though. I am trying to be honest with you. I remember removing my boots, then my socks, leaving them on a step. Scraping my feet through the sand, walking away from the land. I remember thinking how waves have a job to do, how they never tire of wiping the sand, giving it a clean slate, then receding to expose what's underneath. I remember watching some tiny marine creatures and thinking how resilient they had to be, there dogged determination to carry on with what they'd been doing. I admired their, well, for want of a better word, calligraphy, in the sand, it was everywhere. If someone saw me stooping it was because I was taking some time to examine the bubbles that popped from below. David may or may not have been with me right then. I can get so lost inside myself, but still with nature, walking among it, observing everything, but separate from it, just like the seagulls watching everything from a safe distance.

The door opened. A junior officer appeared with two mugs.

"Two sugars please, thank you."

We sipped our tea. It wasn't very nice.

"At first, I thought it was a rock. Then a small seal. Solitary and unmoving at the water's edge, despite the playful nudging by the waves. As I got closer, my heart beat faster. I felt sick. My steps grew heavier. In those moments, you try to tell yourself it can't be."

"Describe in detail what you saw."

"Of course. There was no mistaking a coat, a pair of jeans, deeply saturated, glistening wet hair. I stopped a few feet short. The ears and hands were blueish white.

Then David appeared beside me. I don't know how long it took. He saw what I saw and dropped the coffee cups. He said -

Is he dead?

I couldn't speak at first. I think I just shook my head.

How do you know when someone is definitely dead officer?"

Ds Anderson didn't respond.

"I knew though.

Then I pointed to a place. Half way along the bay there's a 7/11 come post office. Outside the post office I could see a public telephone booth. David said –

What about I wait here and you call for help?

No! I found him, I said. I'm not leaving him now.

I definitely said that.

But David wouldn't move. He froze. Wouldn't budge. So, I had to go myself anyway. Then I went back. He was very pale, I remember.

The police are an hour away, I told him. An ambulance too. They can't say how long. Is the tide coming in do you think? It rather matters a lot right now.

I think I was in shock. They say shock does funny things. I sat down on the wet sand. I just talked to David.

I remember him saying-

So what do we do then Pattie? What do we do?

Well, I'm not leaving him, and there's not much we can do unless we're happy to drag him along the sand, then that might be tampering with evidence. I think we should just wait, maybe get help from the locals. I know what my father would do in this situation, though. He would think ahead, the emergency services will probably want some answers, he would say, use the 5WH Pattie, be prepared for what they might ask, you know, the why, who, what, where, when, and how? Shall we do that?

David laughed. Oh, like, what are we doing here, why were we the ones that found him. Who might be responsible if anyone. Is that what you mean?

Yes.

Oh.

We didn't speak for a while. It was awkward, I don't mind admitting that. Then David piped up.

I was hoping this break would fix us.

I said, Oh. So, the elephant followed us to Coverack after all. I thought about the waves wiping the sand. He was unfaithful to me. I saw a photo once. I imagined her face on the sand, hoping she might be erased, but she was still there when the waves receded.

He said he was sorry.

I just said, I know. But in my mind, she is still here.

Well, he said, shall we give your dad's 5WH a go?

Yes please.

Ok then. Why the hell did we choose this morning, you know, to come out for a stroll? Sorry, but that's what I'm thinking right now.

I remembered my book. An Isabelle Allende novel.

I was reading remember? You tore me away from it because you were restless.

Oh yes.

It was your idea.

Yes. Sorry.

Try again, I say.

He winced. I could see it was getting harder for him to speak.

So, who is he then?

I don't mind telling you, I felt so angry with him right then. Please don't take that to mean I wanted to hurt him.

Angry, why?

David's secret lover, why do you think?

Then what happened?

David was having difficulty breathing, I think he was getting agitated. Stressed. He screamed at me to go and get help but I didn't want to leave him. So, I stayed, and the tide was coming in.

Can I have some water please?"

"In a bit, carry on."

"They found me with David. You told me I was holding a rock. The only reason I can think of was to weigh David down. The water was over my waist and I was holding on. The waves, were pushing, and pulling, almost violently, at the both of us. I thought I would lose him. They just wouldn't let up. Pushing and shoving but also drawing us out. Out to sea. My hands were numb. Blue. My mind was numb. I was freezing. I remember clinging so tightly to his waist. His face was blue, I saw the lights leave his eyes. I thought if I stroked his eyelids and strawberry lashes... But I never saw any blood. Not at any time…if that's what you think.

Then the rescuers came. Grabbed me and grabbed David. They separated us. A young policewoman covered me with a borrowed dry robe. She asked me lots of questions. In my head I was turning a page. I know that nothing I said added up…or would add up. She was a nice young lady, she squeezed my hand and said it was understandable, she explained that this is what shock does."

Anderson let out a deep breath.

"You see why I'm having trouble with this don't you, Patricia? You say yourself, your story doesn't add up."

"I know. I'm sorry for that. Of course it doesn't make sense officer. I told you it was a mess in my head. Of course the body I saw was my husbands. Who else could it be, unless you found two? Would you rather I make things up so they travel in straight lines? Remember what I said about the red herrings? My story is true because it's imperfect. Not the other way round. Liars come up with perfect stories. I am not lying. My father taught me a very important lesson, that the worst people were the ones who could only cope with information that came in black and white. They learned not to trust anything else, he said. People who so desperately need black and white in their lives, they're the same people who wallow in conspiracy theories. My father charged people with actual conspiracies, so he understands the type of scepticism built on stupidity."

"Did you kill David?"

"No."

"You struck him with a rock. Isn't that what happened?"

"Definitely not."

"It's difficult to believe you."

"It is for you, I can see that."

"It'll be difficult for a jury too."

"Why? Because I'm not being logical? Because this doesn't make life easy for you? There is no crime here and you determined to find one, are you not? You don't have to answer that by the way. I can tell you prefer to believe what you do."

Anderson's face was crimson, like a sky on the edge of night. He was raising his voice at me, repeating the same phrase over and over.

"A jury's not going to believe you either."

I was exasperated. My only desire was to help.

"What difference does it make if I made it to the beach first, or David? Perhaps your…witnesses…are right, maybe I was the one who bought two cappuccinos and panicked when I saw him out there. So what? Not that I can agree with that line, but. Perhaps I didn't want to-

accept. That the seal was my husband. At first, I would have thought he was lying down, being a silly bugger, and then I would think, oh no, what with two heart attacks in his pocket already, oh no, oh no. This was the third. I didn't police my husband's medication, officer. I don't know if he took his pills this morning. Isn't that something you can check?"

Clearly, Detective Sergeant Anderson was having a bad day, from which I derived a small amount of satisfaction. I got put back in a cell. A few hours later, I heard the two men close by, sharing their secrets with me again.

"Bail her," a man ordered. "Let's see what the pathologist report has to say."

"I feel I need to make my feelings clear sir, what about the blow to the forehead?"

"Did anyone see her actually strike him?"

Silence. I felt a pang of elation for that silence.

"Well?"

“Not yet. But look. We have motive. The investigation is ongoing. We’ve asked for witnesses.”

“Bail her,” his boss barked.

Twenty minutes later, they let me go, subject to bail.

It must have been 7 o’ clock in the morning when I reached Suntrapped.

Everything in the house looked the same as it had 24 hours ago.

The leaves of the camelias were glowing in the sun. The flowers dying already, gone to join poor David. Little pink buds lay on the ground. I took stock. I felt better. In time I would feel better still. In the conservatory, I saw my Isabelle Allende at one end of the chair, and David’s pair of sandals at the other.

The Weight of a Bell

The men were in the pub, talking loudly.

Luke remained outside in the pub garden, nursing a bottle of Panda Pop which Judd had given him. The raucous laughter of the men, their drunken wisdom, came spilling through the walls. Alcohol performs miracles, Luke thought bitterly. They think their threats are funny, their fists harmless, their presence a shadow. Better to keep a distance, and wait for the inevitable next move.

Dusk came. The men emerged; their faces smug with satisfaction. Judd stumbled out last, his squat frame unbalanced by heavy boots and fists as large as hammers.

His gaze swept the garden like a searchlight, until it fell on Luke.

'There you are.' Judd growled, his mean, pink eyeballs narrowing. A voice both hoarse and jagged, like gravel scraped across a blade.

'Yes sir,' said Luke, his small frame tensed.

'You scared of heights?'

'No sir.'

Judd snorted. 'Mm. Be of no use if you can't climb.'

'I can climb.'

'Mm. You best remember lad. Your ma swore blind,' he mumbled. 'Bigged you up, she did. Promised you'd be no trouble, said you would do anything… Have to say I wasn't so sure until she made certain guarantees. So this is out of the goodness of my heart.'

Guarantees? He didn't dare ask.

Judd's eyes wandered, then set on Luke again. Lit up.

'Well, that's great! Come on then. We're going to work.'

'On foot?' asked Luke.

'Don't be stupid,' said Judd. 'I can drive better drunk than you can walk sober.'

Judd gestured towards his battered Ford Escort, parked crookedly outside the pub.

***

Martin Locke, the tower captain of St Leonard's Church, crouched in the belfry. A lantern flickered. Monday morning. Outside the air was grey and heavy. Above his head, Bell 4, C sharp, loomed silent and still, its clapper wrapped in shadows. To his mind, the Sunday service had gone perfectly, but here he was still.

'Find anything yet?' called Mr Green, Martin's assistant. A stout man in forties, Mr Green preferred the ground level mysteries of wiring to the vertigo inducing climb.

Martin, nimble despite his progressive years, probed the mechanism with care. His fingers, arthritic but precise, were feeling for the clapper bushes, checking for wear and tear and making sure that the clapper staple bolt wasn't loose.

'Spanner,' he muttered eventually, extending a hand.

Only Mr Green's hand appeared from below, holding onto the appropriate spanner. Martin held it to the mechanism, his mind far away, not on the bell, rather on the year it had been forged. 1681. He wondered about the craftsmen who had cast it, their long-forgotten tools shaping metal into music.

'So sorry Martin, about all of this,' Mr Green kept repeating.

When Martin finally descended, a streak of oil in his long white hair gave him the look of a weary wizard.

'Tell Mrs Green we've had a look,' he said. 'But if she still claims it's misbehaving, it might just be her ear.'

'Yes Martin.' There was a pause. "But what if it is her ear?'

***

Recently, theft had plagued St Leonard's. Incidents of vandalism to the headstones, then lead going from the roof. Stained glass fractured. Even sacred places weren't spared.

A handsome young officer arrived, and ticked his way down a form. It took him all of two minutes.

"These things come in waves," he concluded.

Reverend Joyce Matthews vented her frustrations to Martin in the nave, her usually bright demeanour clouded.

"They've taken everything Mr Locke. It wasn't enough we were already crumbling. Now we're leaking too. And the insurance company, well, they're about as useful as a teapot made of chocolate."

Martin began a count of the various pots and pans scattered around to catch the leaks.

"What will you do?" he asked.

'What can I do in all honesty? You know, I was thinking, in case they come back, of camping overnight. Maybe with a bottle of wine for company. I do believe they call that glamping these days?'

Martin smiled and placed a fatherly hand over hers.

'Hm. Just the idea of you being here alone while a gang of criminals tries to break in.'

Maureen, a church volunteer in her sixties, tip toed inside and quietly placed a tray on a pew, cups of afternoon tea and a small plate piled with bourbon biscuits. For Martin's benefit, she gave a wink and a smile, then stealthily slipped away again. As bell captain, Martin had an ex officio role within the Parochial Church Council. As a rule, he did not attend the regular Parish Council Meetings; the casual conversations afforded by the Reverend were long-established, a way for the Reverend to let off steam. The biscuit allocation on these occasions was more generous too.

Martin watched the Reverend's lips as she spoke, his gaze then drawn to streaks of coloured light filtering through the high windows. Dust particles danced about her in the air, jolted by the Reverend's exasperated sighs.

Joyce glanced at him, her expression softening. "What are you thinking?"

"I was wondering," Martin said, "how much dust a person breathes in a lifetime."

She blinked. Then laughed—a clear, chiming sound that reminded him why the parish loved her so.

***

Luke arrived at St Leonard's unannounced, his heart thudding as he approached the tower. He'd heard the bells before, their voices bold and mysterious, calling him like an unfinished sentence.

When Reverend Matthews found him waiting, she directed him to the bell captain, who raised a quizzical eyebrow, then told Luke to wait a while.

It was the first time Luke had seen the inside of St Leonards by day. The light revealed colour, intricacy, a wealth of old things. He was drawn to a tall trio of stained-glass windows, mainly reds and blues interspersed with yellow, each of them a cartoon like depiction of Jesus. Baby Jesus, Jesus the grown-up, surrounded by people who craved his touch. Finally, Jesus giving comfort to someone lying ill in bed. How lovely it would be, he thought, to wake every morning to the light of such windows.

Martin and Mr Green appeared.

“Are you the one who wants to ring the bells?” Mr Green said sternly.

‘His name is Luke,’ said Martin.

The boy nodded quietly.

Martin studied the boy, noting his small hands and anxious eyes. “Well as bell captain, I am very happy to see some young blood showing an interest like yours. So. What do you say? Happy to have a go, Luke?” he said.

Up in the tower, Luke took his place at the rope. Martin explained the rhythm, and Lizzie, one of the ringers, demonstrated.

“Ready, lad?” Martin asked.

Luke nodded, his hands trembled as he gripped the sally. Martin gave the signal and then with all his might, he pulled. The rope resisted at first, then yielded as the bell swung. On the fifth pull, a low, resonant *dang!* filled the air. Luke realised he was grinning. A grin which widened with each chime.

Dang! Dang! Dang!

The bell was alive in his hands—a heavy, willing partner. For the first time in his life, Luke felt strong enough to command something vast.

***

It was the middle of summer. Luke crept into the chapel to find Martin lighting a tall brown candle and rooting it in a base of sand. Martin heard the boy shuffle and turned to face him.

“Sir,” he said.

Martin looked surprised. Luke bit his lip, wondering whether he’d made a mistake coming here, and if it was better to make a quick exit.

‘It’s okay.’ said Martin. ‘I am lighting this one for James. My son.’

‘He’s dead?’ said Luke, inching further closer.

'A long time ago. It feels like yesterday sometimes.'

The boy felt sad for the man he had come to respect.

Martin picked up a new candle and held it out.

'Here,' he said, 'There must be someone you'd like to light this for?'

Luke rummaged his pockets for loose change, then shied away, looking at Martin as though he had remembered his own pain.

'What's wrong?' asked Martin.

'I can't,' Luke said glumly, 'I only have bad money.'

*

Summer deepened, but darkness lingered in Luke's life. Judd had assumed the role of stepfather, and was relentless in his control of both Luke and his mother.

"Clent's roof," Judd said one evening, his voice low with menace. "I know you have a fondness, but you'll go, or I'll make sure you can't go nowhere."

Luke, emboldened by his time at the church, was defiant. "No."

Judd's response was swift and brutal. He slammed the boy to the ground, his fingers tightening around Luke's throat. The world blurred for Luke as darkness claimed him.

Somewhere in the distance, the bells of St. Leonard's began to ring. Their sound was clear, deliberate.

One…two…three.

The toll for a child.

Four…five…six.

The toll for a woman.

Seven…eight…nine.

For a man.

Ludd's grip slackened. His men were watched on in a state of shock. They just stood there, pale and silent. Luke gasped for air, his body trembling.

"Remember this," said Judd to his men as he rose from the ground. "The lot of you. You best remember.'

***

Luke never returned that summer. Despite the short time he had spent at St Leonards, the bell ringers missed him, including Mr Green, but Martin particularly. Luke had left his mark. Each bell had been given its own name now, from A to G, Alfie up to Gordon. Greatly thanks to the boy.

"He reminded me why I keep ringing," Martin confessed to Joyce one day. "Everyone has their own reasons. But for me, the bells are more than sound. They're messages—prayers—echoing through time. When I ring, I feel..., well...I know...I'm speaking to my son."

Joyce smiled, placing a hand over his.

She was back to herself. She had not had to camp overnight. CCTV had been installed, courtesy of Mr Green, who added an alarm system into the bargain.

The bells of St. Leonard's continue to ring, their voices a constant in the lives of the villagers. To some, they are music. To others, they are memories. For a boy named Luke, who hears them from time to time, they are a reminder of a moment when he felt weightless, lifted by something. Something greater than himself.

Arina

Summer 2021
Sixteen years have passed, and it feels so raw. She had had time to steel herself, preparing herself mentally while the car climbed the winding roads up to Agios Giorgos church, a little outside the village of Katastari. Despite it all her heart is racing, hands trembling. It is a hot afternoon. Apart from the driver and her, there is no-one else around.

Pamela exits from an air-conditioned car into the rising heat of the day. A little uncomfortable, not yet unbearable. Not yet a wall of heat. The view always, and is, immediately breathtaking. The sky with its deep-sea blueness. The church with its tall white expansiveness. The wispiness of the sea. In Greece, the colours of the Greek national flag are everywhere.

The church is elevated from the ground by a thick concrete plinth that bisects an extensive graveyard. Once upon a time the builders were faced with a choice, and clearly preferred building the plinth to excavating hard mountain rock for the foundations. The church appears much younger than the curtilage of old stones.

After passing through an iron gate, and the driver tracing her path from a respectful distance, she moves towards the steps that lead to the church. She strains her neck. A tall heavy oak door to the church towers over her, the belltower even more. The driver sidles past and has a go at the oak door, looks back and shakes his head. He skirts the walls for another entrance. The glare of the white hurts the eyes. The terracotta roof glows red. Tall arched windows sit unreachably from both south and north facing walls. The driver returns, still shaking his head.

Pamela moves quietly and thoughtfully through the weeds. Far below eye level, cars and boats crawl noiselessly in all directions. As it is meant to be, day to day life is elsewhere, framed beautifully by tall mountain slopes to the rear, and the gentler plains which fall towards the sea. This land is a land she loves, made of olive groves and red tiled houses, punctuated by tall pointed cypress trees and curved pines.

The ground here is hard and flat, populated by rectangular marble graves of various years and sizes, separated by lush green vegetation. Her legs get heavier with each moment, because they take her to a plot that stands apart from the others, the width of four bodies placed side by side. They are still here. Of course they are. Cemented in time. A translucent marble surround, small white stones to cover them, a cross bearing the family name overlooking them. Four photographs equally spaced, protected by Perspex sheet. Each depicting a solemn face. Like, did they know the fate to become them? Surely not. She knew them well. She can see them in her mind. The real people they were, how they used to call out to one another. *Arina! Fanis! Come! Come!*

Yes. Gone since God knows how long. But their voices very much alive.

Spring 2003

May comes and just like spring flowers the tourists begin to appear, here and there. Pamela sits on a wooden bar stool in a small work shed, her hands ready in waiting, for her brain to tell them to begin her sand art. Pamela's partner

Christos had encouraged her to have a go. *You can do this.* Through his friend now turned her friend, Arina, she got permission to use the shed, positioned in one corner of the sea front taverna, which she now thought of as her studio. Not ordinarily a tidy person, Pamela's shed is stacked with pots and plates, bottles, and jars, all of which have enjoyed previous lives. Near to hand are glues, brushesm and a variety of coloured sands. For some reason her hands are trembling. At first, passers-by and customers using the taverna, look her way as she works, making her feel exposed. *Come on, I can do this.*

After a while, thankfully, the nerves subside at the realisation that this is a new adventure.

Across the yard there are five steps leading up to the taverna, where she can spot the rounded shapes of Arina's parents, Papou Tasos and Nota, both sat at the staff table, their heads in collusion, their location close to the serving counter. Averaging sixty, they tend to take a back seat with the business, though always ready to give a lending hand should it get too busy. Vagelis, Arina's husband, a willowy man with dark hair, hairy limbs, and an impossibly slim waist, takes charge of the kitchen and the cash till. Somehow, he manages to perform all related tasks in white designer clothing without getting them spoiled. In the quieter moments, when he is not barking orders, he sits outside the front of the house, conversing loudly with some Albanian friends. Arina, a gentle natured woman in her early 30s, moves quietly around the gift shop, always on standby in case the taverna gets overloaded.

When business is slow, Arina hops across to visit Pamela, knowing there is a good chance she will also find her 8-year-old son Fanis there. Fanis loves to watch Pamela at work, and quickly offered himself up as her little helper, a job that entails suggesting designs and choosing colours. Arina finds comfort in this new friendship for her son.

One day, while Fanis was out playing somewhere, Arina paid Pamela a call. Pamela downed tools at the sight of her friend, ready for a chat. Arina invited Pamela to take a walk with her along the beach. It was unusual for Arina to leave her area of work, so it must have been important.

'Please Pammy-mou, I only have half an hour and it's a chance to for us to talk.'

'Ok,' said Pamela, rising from her workbench.

Arina stopped her friend before they left the shed.

'Pammy," she said anxiously.

'Yes?'

'In case my husband asks, would you tell him that it was you who wanted to speak to me? Maybe say it was something personal?'

'Of course,' said Pamela. 'Shall we?'

They were barely out the door, ready to commence their beach walk, when Arina's husband called to her.

In that instant, Pamela saw Arina's whole demeanour alter. As if her whole body just froze. Arina visibly took a moment to regain her composure.

'Wait please," she said to Pamela.

Arina turned to go back to the restaurant where Vagelis was waiting at the top of the steps. When she got within reach, he stretched a hand and passed her a mobile phone.

She received it with a smile, and went back to where Pamela was waiting.

It was a horrible thing to witness.

Silently, the two of them walked away, across a dusty road, over a small wall and down some steps that led to the beach, waiting until they were sure they were out of earshot.

'This phone is so he can call me if I am not back in half an hour. I am married to a man with a very dark heart.'

Pamela felt an increasing sense of dread but remained silent. Somehow, she could still feel Vagelis' eyes on them as they strolled off.

On reaching another taverna, a reasonable distance from what was home, Arina suggested they enjoy a coffee. She pointed to a quiet table and they sat down. Arina broke the spell.

'Our wedding was a farce Pammy mou. He said he would kill me if I didn't marry him. It sounds so stupid. But I really didn't know what to do at the time. Now he threatens to kill Fanis if I try to leave, and to make me watch while he does it.'

Pamela was taken aback.

'My God Arina. Do your parents know of this?'

'Some of it. Not all. They are tired Pammy, they're tired of me too. I don't blame them really. Because when I've summoned the courage to leave on previous occasion, and there have been a few, for some stupid reason I kept coming back. You know, they never wanted me to marry him in the first place.'

Pamela held out a hand across the table.

'You probably know. I take medication for depression,' Arina went on, telling her about how Vagelis had taken charge of all her medication, and had taken to dispensing it to her late at night.

Pamela nodded. It was something she had already half suspected. They sipped their coffee quietly, trying their best to soak in the beauty of the Mediterranean Sea.

'Pammy mou.'

'Yes.'

'Should anything happen to me, will you promise me that you will let the world know I was not mad?'

The pain was clearly evident in Arina's eyes. What could Pamela say to this? She merely nodded. They held hands. Arina squeezed them tightly, almost as if she was grateful to have received this oath, as well as relieved.

Half an hour later, as if an alarm had been set, the phone Vagelis had handed to her rang, and they hastily returned to the taverna.

The house behind the taverna

There were no more walks after that. Further conversations mostly took place in Pamela's shed. Arina's confidence had engendered some feeling of responsibility and Pamela couldn't help feeling closer to Arina the more time passed.

Her friend had lots of other qualities. She exuded elegance and a natural beauty. The way she dressed, the way she moved, her choices of clothes, it seemed effortless. Yet very simple, intuitively smart and nicely co-ordinated. When Arina smiled, a youthful beauty blossomed in her cheeks, a generosity showed in her eyes which everyone including Pamela found infectious. Arina enjoyed and asked questions about Pamela's expression of creativity with her artwork, while at the same time encouraging her to grow. Arina was one of the few islanders Pamela could properly talk to. She loved Arina's Greek-ness, one only partially ironed out by an unmistakeable Australian accent, and her straightened yet still full-bodied dark hair.

Beneath Arina's brightness, there was a sadness which she couldn't disguise. Pamela so wanted to help her friend find happiness. There seemed to be only one solution however. One time, Arina explained about her past to her confidant.

'Both Papou Tasos and Nota were born on Zante. But Papou Tasos is not my real father. When I came to Zante from Melbourne, I was 7. My mother told me it was a holiday where I could finally meet my Greek relations.'

'I was so excited Pammy mou. I felt so special being the one chosen to go to Greece and not my big sister. What my mother did not tell me was that she he left my father and her real plans were to return to her place of birth permanently. Can you believe it? When I said my goodbyes to my father and sister, I was in complete innocence, not knowing that this was a final farewell and that many years would pass before I saw them again.'

'The taverna and the house are the only home I have ever known here. Hah! If you could only see what it was back then. Pammy mou, I went from all the comforts and luxuries you might expect in a city like Melbourne, to a house with no electricity, no running water, no heating. No television. No radio. Not even street lighting. Worst of all. I knew no one, I couldn't speak Greek at first either. As a consequence, my youth was spent in utter despair and loneliness.'

Pamela could understand her friend, she herself had developed a dread of entering the family house. A sizeable bungalow situated behind the taverna on the same plot of land, it felt oppressive from the start. The first time she dared to visit, it seemed like the husband was always just a step or two away, following closely wherever Pamela went.

Only once was he out somewhere, leaving the two of them alone in the house, and Arina, desperate to talk, seized the moment.

'Follow me Pamela, there is something I need to show you.'

Pamela followed her friend to the kitchen. Behind the cooker was a sparse wall, with nothing but a meat cleaver hanging from it. It looked ominous by itself.

'What husband buys this… **thing**… as a gift for his wife and hangs it there? I will tell you Pammy mou, this **thing** is to remind me what will happen if I try to leave.'

Pamela felt a deep chill in her spine.

'Pammy mou, I know I can talk to you.'

'Yes, yes…you can...and like-wise…that goes for me Arina.'

'Pamela. You know. All my life I have taken pills for depression. Though now my husband has taken over what I take and when I take it. Can you believe it?'

Fanis

One morning, Pamela was bury in the shed, trying to figure out her next piece of work, when that cute skinny kid appeared at the entrance. Tanned and dark, coupled with a gentle nature, Fanis was the apple of his mother.

'What are you doing?' he asked with an Aussie twang.

'Hi Fanis. I think I'm stuck. I was just wondering if you might be able to help.'

The boy inched closer, saw there was no work in progress, then smiled. Pamela found herself smiling too.

'What's going on?' he asked.

'Well. I thought today I would do a clock with some ladybirds on it, but you know what?'

'No. Tell me'

'Well, I've completely forgotten what ladybirds look like. Can you believe that? Aren't I silly?'

Fanis giggled, 'Yes you are." Then he had a thought which made his face light up. "Wait here. I know what to do.'

He was gone in a flash. Pamela loved that boy.

Minutes later he was back at the door.

'Look,' he said, eyes beaming.

He held out the palm of his hand. A toy ladybird rested upon it. He proceeded to carry out a small demonstration for her.

'Look Pammy, you can open and close its wings.'

Thursday 30th September

It had just turned dark when there was a knock at Christos and Pamela's place. Pamela opened the door to find Arina standing there, looking distraught. She hurried past and pulled the door shut quickly behind her.

'I have run away, I have run away,' the expression on her face was one of terror.

'How did you get here?' Pamela asked.

'I walked. It was the longest walk of my life'

'Where – is – he – Arina?'

'Right now, he is with friends on his computer, I had to do it now. I had to. He's been watching me all day. I think something bad, very bad, was going to happen tonight, I knew I had to do it now.'

Christos and Pamela exchanged glances, they had already talked about this possibility and readily agreed that Arina could stay with them.

'We must go out though,' said Christos with some urgency in his voice, and already fiddling with his next cigarette. 'This is dangerous. We must be seen out. I am sure he will come here first once he knows she has gone.'

Pamela made up a bed on the couch and made Arina promise that under no circumstance was she to open the door or turn on a single light. They closed the shutters and left, leaving Arina alone.

Christos made a few laps of the main roads so that the two of them could be seen around the villages. First down to the beach road and the bars, knowing that Vagelis' Albanian sidekicks, particularly the shadier ones, would have the chance to take note. Then they did the rounds along the main roads, past the main bars, shops and restaurants. It must have been 2 a.m. before they got back home.

Arina answered the door, waiting for them. Eagerly, she showed them a short letter she had prepared for her son, detailing how everything would be OK. She passed it to Pamela, asking her to get it to Fanis via Nota, Arina's mother. They knew it was only a matter of time before they would be discovered, and that it wasn't sensible for Arina to stay with them any longer.

Christos had hatched a plan, and soon departed with Arina, on a mission to find her an inconspicuous place to stay. He drove to Zakinthos town. The streets were dark and less populated now. Eventually he found a vacancy at a small side road hotel, away from nosy villagers.

'Arina,' he said, 'Listen carefully. You must not call home from the hotel, OK? I will bring you a mobile tomorrow that can't be tracked.'

Arina nodded.

Friday 1st October

The next day, Christos and Pamela had the job of getting the letter to Nota. It wasn't without risk. As they turned on to the beach road the sun was rising. Pamela spotted Papou Tasos out in the water in a little blue and white boat, a fishing net hanging over one side. It was almost magical, a gentle mist rose from the sea, the surface of the sea was so still Pamela felt she could walk across it to greet him. Christos slowed the car down and they waved to him. Papa Tasos noticed and waved back.

After, they turned into the drive of the house and knocked on the door. It was very early but Nota and Fanis were known to be early risers. Pamela removed the letter from her bag but as the door opened it was not Nota, but Arina's husband standing there, with a fierce look in his eyes and the sharp movement of a man who is extremely agitated.

Pamela hurriedly tucked the letter back in the bag.

'Is Nota in?' said Christos.

'Yes, but she is not well enough to come to the door. Before you go, I know you know where my wife is.'

They hesitated, stuck for what to say.

Before they could respond, Vagelis shut the door in their faces.

They left in a hurry, agreeing to go straight home. Later, Pamela returned to work, deciding it best to carry on as normal, hoping it might help dispel the husband's suspicions that they were in some way involved. Despite that, it was still a tense day. Pamela didn't get the chance to see Arina's parents that day, nor did she see little Fanis. It felt as though the letter was burning in her bag. She closed her studio early and Christos arrived to pick her up. Pamela got in the car, but before Christos returned to the driver seat his mobile went off. He paced along the footpath up and down while he talked. The tone of his voice was tense. When he finished the call and got in the car Pamela asked him what that was all about. Christos shrugged his shoulders.

'Nothing. Bloody stupid. Vagelis asked me what my last name was.'

While Pamela had been working, Christos sorted out a phone for Arina. Pamela put together a bag of food and assorted toiletries, to go with the new phone on the table.

They waited till dark before daring to leave the house. It was almost 8 in the evening before they were confident enough to go, but just then their front door was pushed open. In rushed Vagelis with Fanis by his side. Without a word he plopped himself down at their kitchen table and immediately began toying with the phone Chris had obtained for Arina.

Pamela froze, 'Is everything Ok?' she asked dumbly.

'Where is she?' he demanded.

"Who, Arina?' said Christos, trying to remain calm, 'That's funny because Pamela mentioned she hadn't seen her at all today either.'

Vagelis glared at them, his chest heaving.

Then little Fanis spoke, 'Papa, look.'

Vagelis rose quickly and followed Fanis to the doorway of the lounge. Fanis pointed towards the couch. Scrunched-up sheets previously used by Arina were still lying there. Vagelis glared at them both, his eyes brimming with hate, then he grabbed Fanis by the arm and stormed out, not uttering a word. They watched as the two hurried down the stairs and climbed onto a motorbike. In the dark, Fanis was illuminated by a small and bright yellow Paddington Bear mackintosh. He turned, smiled, and waved to Pamela as the bike sped off. They disappeared into the night.

The situation was very bad. Time was a kind of agony for Christos and Pamela as they waited another two hours before daring to get to Arina. But eventually they had to risk it, and they went out in the car, keeping their eyes on the road behind them in case they were followed. They reached Zakinthos town without seeing anything suspicious, then walked from a remote street to the hotel. Arina was overjoyed to see them and told them she had used the hotel phone but only to call her sister Maria.

'I went out but only briefly.' She reassured them. 'I was desperate for water. But don't worry. I went out very early and to the first place that was open. Then I came straight back.'

Pamela passed her the bag of things she had prepared.

She needed to take a second look at her friend. For the first time in what seemed forever, Arina was relaxed and smiling.

‘This is my new beginning,’ she said. Her youthfulness back on show.

They had coffee, raised their cups to her new life, and laughed a lot.

They discussed how they were going to get Arina off the island to where she had family on the mainland.

‘It will be difficult because my husband will have people watching the port,’ said Arina.

“You won’t be able to take a boat directly to Athens,” said Christos. “I have an idea.”

They agreed that the best way forward would be to book a tourist excursion to Olympia and somehow hide her amongst the foreigners. After some reflection, Arina said, “I think that might work you know. But do you mind if I run the idea past my sister first. I promise I will let you know as soon as I can tomorrow.”

They hugged each other tightly before leaving. Pamela felt a great weight had come off her chest, there was no need to worry any more. She and Christos went back to their village for a drink at a taverna to celebrate. After a frantic last 24 hours, things began to feel more normal finally. Christos was more his old self, the man Pamela fell in love with. He was an old man but you’d never know it. A serial smoker and drinker, with his zest for life and dancing on tables when there was music, the self that had earned him a reputation on the island as Crazy Christos. The two of them felt such palpable relief they didn’t arrive home until much later.

Saturday 2nd October 2004

A phone rang. It was barely 7 am. They were in bed. Neither of them were ready to face the world yet. It kept ringing. Pamela decided she wasn’t going to answer it, but Christos got up anyway. She listened in a half sleep.

Christos was talking calmly, agreeing with whatever was being said at the other end of the line. After he placed the phone down he came back to bed.

'That was Arina, she says that everything is going to be OK. And she spoke to her sister.'

'Mmm. That's good."

"And Vagelis."

"Oh. What?'

'Her sister said Arina's husband called her and said he's had enough of the situation, and that if Arina pays him 20,000 euros, he will leave the house and the island, but first he needs to talk to Arina in person...'

Pamela felt the room go dark and cold.

'Please say she's not doing that…'

Christos looked hesitant.

'I don't know. She says he is picking her up from the hotel at 9 this morning.'

Pamela shot out of bed, "No. This is not good. No..... No. No… No!"

Christos looked bewildered.

Pamela ran to her phone and called Arina. She picked up immediately.

'Hello.'

'Arina. Listen to me. Christos just told me. You have to run, run, run, run, run. Please. Get out of the hotel now. Please. Just run, run to anywhere and hide."

Arina's voice came back calmly.

"Stamata. Stamata, Pammy-mou, it is OK."

"How does he even know where you are?"

"I tried to ring him on the phone you gave me but it wouldn't work. Did Christos tell you about the money? I was so happy that he is going to leave I rang him on the hotel phone. He must have rung back the number and found which hotel it is.'

Pamela felt numb. Helpless.

'Oh my God Arina, my love, you have to get out of the hotel.' Pamela was begging her.

"I will wait Pammy."

There was a confidence in Arina's voice that didn't reflect the situation, and none of Pamela's words seemed to have any impact.

'Get out now,' she repeated. 'Just get out of the hotel now, please get out.'

'Pammy-mou it is OK, he is coming with the police, and our son."

Pamela took a few seconds to digest this.

"Yes. But are you sure the police will be there?"

"Yes. He promised me. They will be with him."

"Oh Arina, please my love, leave. This is…it sounds so wrong."

"Tch. It will be OK, I'll call you when I get home."

Pamela's mind was racing.

"Arina before you go, please hide the phone we gave you, he saw it when he came to the house and if he sees you with it, he will know that we helped you."

"I will Pammy-mou, you will see. Everything will be fine. We will speak later."

Then the line went dead.

By the time their phone rang again, it was early afternoon. Arina was at the other end. She began by saying she was back home and that her son was listening to the call so he could translate what was being said to his Dad.

'OK,' said Pamela warily.

'Pammy-mou…you know that thing that we spoke about earlier, well he has it.'

Pamela pictured the phone they didn't want Vagelis to see. It was too late now.

'Don't worry Arina, it was no big deal.'

Arina's voice had lost the lightness from the night before. It was much more deliberate.

'No…that thing…he has it.'

'Don't worry, how are you, is everything OK?'

'Yes, my husband wants you and Christos to come down later so we can all have a drink.'

Pamela hesitated.

'I'm not sure Arina, let me think about it and call you back.'

'He really does want you both to come down, it'll be nice.'

'Let me ask Christos, ok? He's not here right now. I promise I will get back to you.'

Arina seemed reluctant to end the call, but there didn't appear to be anything else to say, so the call ended.

Pamela went across to Christos, who was laid out on the couch watching TV.

'Everything OK?'

'I don't know, Chris. Something in her voice – wasn't right. Anyway, she said Vagelis wants us to go down later and have a drink with them. Don't you think that's weird? Up until now we haven't been welcomed anywhere near the house, let alone enter it."

Christos looked up at her. He was tired, worn out by the whole affair.

'I don't want to go down there. I definitely don't want to see him.' He said.

Pamela felt the same. They agreed not to go.

Sunday 3rd October 2004

Sunday morning was a beautiful morning in Alykanas. A calm Ionian Sea. The village still half asleep. No whisper of a breeze, but still cool. In sharp contrast, the road along the front of the taverna was crammed with vehicles, police and ambulance, their emergency lights flashing. Yellow tape was stretched across various access points, the side path to the house, the steps up to the taverna. To the man who would take charge, officer Karaganis, it seemed there were enough men there just to guard the tape. A definite 'No go' for the public. A crime scene just hours old. His mental processes were whirring. Facts are still being gathered, but already they total an autumnal nightmare. What was four, has quickly risen to five bodies. How many shots were reported? This will need to be checked again. A local officer leads him through the house behind the restaurant, room by room. The faces of his colleagues are busy, serious, sombre and pale. Also eager to prove themselves. It takes real effort to fix on what they are trying to tell him, their take on the bodies and the sequence of events. Theories already abound. The murder weapon has been found. A shotgun belonging to the family. He prays he can keep his head in this moment, apply what needs to be done according to the homicide manual. Throughout the house there is a trail of blood linking the bodies. Along the floors, across the walls, a macabre abstract that cannot and will never be unseen.

The police radio crackles. Karaganis will have to update his superiors shortly. Inevitable that a crime of this magnitude will go national. Become a circus even. A nine-year old boy, such a tragedy. The father mixed up with local drug gangs, though not substantiated as part of these crimes. A crazy wife. Everything must be preserved and dissected before a sensible and reasonable conclusion can be arrived at. It is his crime scene. He understands the importance of amassing as many details as possible in the first 24 hours. There can be no room for complacency, despite having on the face of it, the victim, the victims, the crime scene, and the suspect, all in one place. That is what the manual says to focus on. Victim. Scene. Offender. Keep the mind focussed on that. They are all here. His thoughts are interrupted by a tap on the shoulder. Another colleague, shaking with excitement and apprehension, hands him a note. What now?

‘Look, he says. ‘It is handwritten, see what it says? It implicates Crazy Christos.’

By the time Christos and Pamela visited the taverna that morning, the whole area had been cordoned off by police. They felt such a wave of shock and horror they spun around and went home right away. But at home there was no respite and they only felt more restless. Christos paced around until he determined he had to go back to find out more. When he returned, he was fighting back the tears.

‘They’ve all gone, all gone Pamela. He killed them all - and then himself.’

‘That’s it then,” Pamela said resignedly. “We must go to the police about this.’

She picked up the phone and punched in a number. When she got through to the station, an officer told her they were busy, took some details and said they would call if they needed to speak to them. Less than an hour later the police called back and summoned them to the station. On arrival they were placed in a large noisy room with many other people. Pamela noticed a gun being bandied about in a far corner of the room, at least four men were handling it with intense curiosity.

After a long wait an officer waved to Pamela and Christos and beckoned them to a private room where they faced a series of questions. Pamela stressed that Arina had gone to the police for help, but said she had been turned away. The officer said he would check the records but came back saying there was no report to back up that claim. The questioning revolved more about what she knew about drugs on the island.

Summer 2021

It was strange for Pamela. Standing above her friends in the grave, hearing their voices as though it were yesterday. **Papou Tasos** (Yiannis), 63, **Nota** (Panaiota), 58, **Arina**

(Arina Panaiota), 34, **Fanis** (Fanis junior), 9. The Zantiotis family.

She knew, especially, that Arina's words the day at the café would be etched in her head forever. A cry for help. And then calamity. And after all these years, why did it remain so hard?

'…you will let the world know that I was not mad.'

'I know. I know," she says to the sky and the mountains.

Now where is my driver?

She pulls her gaze away from Arina's and sees him meandering between some other gravestones.

I feel I can trust him.

Why?

He said he would like to write about this, Arina. Or at least, give it a go. What do you think?

Last Stop

On or off, like switches we are. Stand and live, sit and die. I thought about giving up within a few hours of leaving Warsaw, I could hardly think of anything else. Dying doesn't seem so bad, the further we go. My chest hurts. The coughing has stopped for now. I keep thinking. Why am I here? I am not a proper Jew.

"You think that will save you?" scoffed an old woman. Sometimes I think aloud.

"How much further?" I say to anyone, but mainly to the man who looks like he used to be a bank clerk. All professions temporarily discarded for now.

"You're not from Warsaw?" he asks, like that's bad.

"Athens," I say.

"Ah."

"You didn't answer my question."

"He is not a proper Jew," a voice stressed, from somewhere I couldn't see.

The bank clerk looked at me.

"Soon." He says, annoyed. He can hardly speak, his throat is a metal file, and smells like a dead fish.

No one has water. We lick our sweat. He is shorter than me, and his build, in Greek we would say the word *kontostoupis*, meaning short and plump. I am rakish, according to my mother, built like a 'Meccano' set. When the train departed, my left elbow occasionally dug into the bank clerks ribcage. At first he reacted, we tussled, he pushed back, but after a time we melded. His chest has adjusted and we are a snug fit. I ask where we are going, shouldn't a bank clerk know these things? He repeats he doesn't know. It's a straight track. Someone must know. He cannot have been very competent at the bank. I persist with the question, that's all I can do.

An alto male voice calls from a corner of the carriage. 'East'. I don't want to hear this, no one does. East is bad. There have been stories, too fantastic. I don't want to hear them. "East", the voice calls again. No. No. Someone make them quiet.

The livestock is moody. "Shut up!" It cries. That is the last time we hear Mr Alto.

The carriage, which has become an oven, heated by humans, heaves and billows with baked flesh. Strangers push against one another like awkward lovers. Personal space is the thickness of a shirt or a blouse, a dress or trousers. Not enough. We have become familiar, lost some of our shyness. I don't belong here.

"Good for you. Do you think anyone here does?" Oh dear. Thinking aloud again.

I alter my orientation several times, somewhere there must be a friendly face, a look not steeped in self-misery. I turn about, slowly through 360 degrees. I see you. Beaten faces, hungry faces, faces from which the soul has already flown. I settle on the young woman next to me, her back has stayed toward me since we were put on this truck. From her dark brown hair, I extrapolate to exquisite shoulders and waist. There was a life before all of this, a time when I would have cowered before daring to speak to such beauty.

I haven't seen her face in all this time, yet I can tell it will be the most wonderful face I have ever seen. Even in the absence of light, or the ability for me to see.

"What is your name?" I ask.

She says nothing but still I watch. She breathes with her entire body, shoulders rise, then fall, hair moving gently across her back. The air drowns in the stench of human waste but it cannot touch her. She dips to speak quietly to the ear of an elderly gentleman who nods a white moustache up and down. Perhaps her uncle or something. He stares at everything suspiciously. What do I have to do to see her? She doesn't engage with me, and yet, I know she doesn't mind us being so close. She could have moved if she had wanted. Last night, last night, oh yes, last night, when the rules changed. Darkness brought anonymity despite our mental maps. I nestled my face in her thick frizzy hair. Even under my paltry weight, her body stared to sink and reacted swiftly to raise her back up. I whispered an apology and stood strong and upright for a time. Then I forgot myself and did it again. And again. This is how lovers move if they have to sleep upright, half asleep like horses. Am I right?

That's it! A stable of horses, creatures who once roamed free, made love, and made choices. Forgive my rambling.

Male to female, female to male, male to male. Is there a right way? I don't know. I ache, ache, ache for an answer. "How do you choose?" I think aloud in the dark. "Shhhhsh", a snake hisses back. There are snakes here now. Is it because I am not a proper Jew? You are not a proper Jew, but you're going with them anyway.

They were right. How could I be? I am Greek. A Greek boy who got caught passing through Italy.

How to stand for hours, it's impossible. Like others I've seen, I practice, call it an experiment, letting my weight go, first on one leg, then the other, then with both to see if the compression could be enough to keep me upright, it is not. The carriage shakes and bumps from side to side and inevitably you slide. Bodies immediate to you take notice when they sense it, pulling away. Fall, their movement tells you. Just don't take me with you. There is no shame in it. I don’t blame them. No-one close to me has fallen, not even the bank clerk, though I have wished it on him several times. Which of us should fall first?

Morning comes and summer sunlight flashes through the tiny cracks of our wooden cage, teasing the eyes. The train is fickle. It stops nowhere then moves in short spurts. We are moving, and then it feels like we are moving, when we hear the sound of another train passing in the opposite direction. Such deception. A train passes along another track, invisible to the eye, imparting sounds and vibrations, then goes away, but I can hear it moving with ease. Such luxury.

Sometimes just an inch at a time, pause, so we can act like mice. Yes. From humans to horses, horses to snakes. Snakes to mice. Listen! Are we there yet? No. It's just the guards shouting outside, *Keine Angst, Keine Angst.* Oh wait! Yes. We are here. Oh sorry. My mistake. I only thought…*W*hy shouldn’t we be afraid if we choose to live? For no apparent reason the journey resumes.

If I fall to the floor, I won’t ever rise up again, it is a fact. The space I leave will fill. I know myself. I lack the strength to push back against them, I lack the violence necessary to regain my position. If the young woman would agree to fall with me too. The thought of resting on the floor with her appeals like cool water, clear and sweet. I don't care what the reality might be. I haven’t been down there yet to see but I can imagine. That world. Forests of legs and shoes, bare feet, a landscape coloured with blood, shaped by excrement, valleys irrigated by rivers of piss, suitcases for buildings, the land of the dead young and old, an airless hell and sleeping paradise. Hardly a bed for lovers, but I can reason that maybe it is still not the worst place.

"Please. What is your name?" I repeat when we come face to face, by accident, her lips not so far from mine. I give her my best smile. She is beyond what I had imagined. So young. 16? 17? Her green eyes are wide and open, welcoming. Her cheeks pink and unblemished. I am struck.

Come share my pain and my joy. Your eyes are so deep I can see into you, your strength, your youthfulness, your optimism.

Are you studying me too? Yes. Here I am. I hide nothing. Can you sense my vulnerableness? I want you to see it. I was a student, in Paris, an engineer…I was going home. Her mouth breaks into a smile and turns. I want that mouth on mine so badly.

Well! *If you won't tell me your name, I shall call you Amira.* Well, I think to myself, that's a good Jewish name. It hints of love. I slide my free arm around her waist, she is startled and I feel her hand go to grab mine. I expect her to yank it away, instead she grips it so tightly it hurts. The she loosens her grip but her hand remains. I am hurting with happiness. If we are still here tonight and I fall then maybe I can pull my lover with me.

Dear God. I wish with all my heart for another night. There is nowhere else I would rather be. Just the chance to press my heart to yours, mine to beat against yours, every second. Our hearts will make love while we stand. No-one will know. It would be enough for me. I could face anything afterwards. Did I tell you how beautiful you are?

The train stutters, screeches, slows. The wheels squeal as though they will surely seize up for the last time. We lurch as one. The carriage halts abruptly. New sounds. New smells. Boots crunching through gravel, amid screams, whistles blow, there is much rage outside. Carriage door locks clank open and shouts of 'schnell.' Amira's hand tightens around mine. She looks for her uncle but he is gone.

He has entrusted you to me. I don't have to say anything. She knows because she stays.

Don't worry my love, everything will be fine. She panics anyway. The light has taken away my ability to speak aloud through mere thought. Better to say something she can hear.

"Soon," I whisper, for her ears only. "Soon we will be able to breathe again."

(This story is for my Godmother Norma Ruffell who was arrested and taken to Auschwitz at the age of 17. By some miracle she survived.)

The Poem

I used to come here with Harry. Remembering comes as waves, gently rocking. I was young, without these responsibilities. Remembering comes from the sea, untouched by years, not in a bottle, but perfectly preserved in the salt water. As though it had been waiting, perhaps treading water, perhaps travelling the world, but waiting out there, all the time.

My new life, my love, is Lily, my partner. It was Lily's idea. Let's go to the beach, she said. This one she said, her finger on a map. Oh no! This is Harry's beach I thought, though I never said it aloud. It was October, I looked out the window and the sun was weak, surrendering to a thick fog. A good reason to stay indoors, I suggested. But Lily insisted, so we drove here anyway.

The car park was empty when we arrived. We walked a little way, down a track, and further down another. So here we are. The mud cliffs high above and behind us, almost invisible. A fog to our front, right and left. The English Channel, I know, out there somewhere, stealthily silent, under the spell of the fog, as quiet as pondwater.

I cast my gaze along what I know, in my right mind, to be shoreline comprised of mainly heavy sand, broken clumps of terracotta mud, and potato sized pebbles. I can't hear the sea. Only the pebbles that crunch underfoot. From left to right, I can barely make out 20 yards of beach.

'I do believe the sea was right there the last time I came,' I said, pointing to nowhere.

'I can't imagine it's gone anywhere,' said Lily. She takes a deep breath. 'Tell me why we've never come here before. It's very exciting don't you think?'

'A little scary, (if you ask me), don't you sense it's like a big wall has closed in and it's like, we're trapped in a room belonging to a stranger.'

'Oh. A large private room, I never thought of it that way', she says, winking, flirting. 'You know what that means though? Oh yes. We can do whatever we want'

'This isn't funny Lil. We could die if we don't keep an eye on the tide.'

Even in the morning gloom, Lily's dark beautiful eyes somehow manage to emit a glint of light. She shakes her hair and tilts at me. She challenges me at the best of times. I love her for that. She laughs a raucous laugh which fills the air, safely contained by the curtain of mist that surrounds us.

'Ah. Tragedy,' she yells. 'Couple found naked. Cause unknown. Inquest pending.'

She senses my unease, and intuitively grabs my hand. I pull away, gently. It is too late. An unwelcome thought beset me. Sprung in my head so quickly I had no time to fend it off. Harry could be out there somewhere. And if he is then he might see us, and I didn't want that. Though I try to wave away such a ridiculous notion, still he haunts me. Harry passed away a year ago. At first, I didn't know. A friend obsessed with social media told me. I missed his funeral.

Lily doesn't know about Harry. What she sees is me pull away, and for that she feigns rejection. Only for a moment. She can't know enough about me to understand why I feel this way. Can she? She begins to strip.

"What are you doing?" I say.

"What does it look like," she says.

'No! We can't,' I say, but in no time she is half undressed.

'Why not silly. No one can see. And even if they could, what would they see?'

Two crazy shadows sliding into the sea. Well. Bums to that.

'I know this beach, Lily. The tides can catch you out. They come in faster than you can imagine.'

'Nonsense! Sh. Just listen.'

'You see? The sea is asleep,' she whispers. "And we can be quiet."

Lily doesn't feel the cold. She is down to her underwear, her back to me, tentatively hobbling across the pebbles towards the water.

'Come on!' she cries. In less than a second, she is gone. 'It's freezing! (She laughs. Her voice grows faint) Come on then,' just a distant voice now, embedded in the mist.

I haven't moved an inch. Even though I cannot see where I am, I know exactly where I am. I met Harry, right here, at this exact spot.

The first time I laid eyes on him, he had created a huge roaring fire from burning wool, entirely from burning wool, wool that had made it ashore in crates. The timber from the crates was too wet to burn, so he'd created a separate pile near to the fire. The pallets bore a large stamp with the words Ceylon and Flammable in red ink. But the wool had been wrapped tightly in waterproof wraps, and was happily ablaze, and the heat was intense. It was a clear night in August, a chill breeze fanned the flames and froze my fingers.

The young man was tall, and wiry. He beckoned me to come and keep warm. I held my hands towards the flames. We watched the tall waves side by side. He pointed to more crates floating in, rolling along the sand, of similar size, they seemed to bear the same markings.

I find stuff all the time, he told me. *Flotsam, or is it jetsam when it's landed? And at what point exactly do you reckon that flotsam becomes jetsam?*

I don't know anything about flotsam or jetsam. I shrugged my shoulders.

When ships lose their cargo, the currents often deliver it to these shores.

His blonde face was brightly illuminated by the flames, I watched his lips as he mouthed words I didn't understand, I swear his eyes were as bright as the stars when they studied me, which made me feel very dizzy. I believe I fell in love at that very moment, because I remember feeling sick at the same time.

Not long after we became lovers. I would say my first proper kiss was in the sea. It was sunny and hot. The currents moved caressingly about our bodies. A lingering salty kiss sustained me for so long the sea must have noticed my neglect, and taken advantage, by catching up with the shore and stealing our bags from where we had left them.

Luckily, our indulgent trance like embrace was broken when an elderly couple called to us from the beach. They kept shouting and gesticulating, saying words we could not hear, excitedly pointing towards an area half way down the beach. I gasped. Our bags were now afloat, a long way from where we had left them, but for now temporarily captive in a rock pool. We waded back as quickly as we could, laughing till it hurt when we were finally able to retrieve them, and then individually compare how fully saturated our clothes and shoes had become.

The fact our bags had remained together during their attempted escape remained a talking point for a long time. The fact that we, as a couple, did not, was a point of reflection that returns to me every so often.

A few years after not seeing each other, we met by chance. We went for a coffee. It was mainly small talk. Not awkward, just unimportant. Until Harry told me he was still writing, and that he'd written a poem. About us. My first thought was, how could he?

Not now, now that we led our lives independent of one another. And my life so different from before. Why dredge up the past? At least read it, he said. So, I did, and as I did, I felt my face burn.

'I can't undo it,' he said stubbornly, 'It's written.'

'You don't understand Harry, it's us. I thought we were an island. I thought we had agreed to stay an island.'

'We are, and we will,' he said, 'And this, this (he waved the poem in the air, in my face) is testament to it.'

An irrational fear grabbed me. 'No. No. Promise me you won't publish this.' I demanded.

We stared into our mugs. At some point among the silence, he said something that remains engrained,

'Olivia. You know how I feel about you, it's in here. In my heart. It shall always be here. But in all the time I've known you, you've practiced three forms of tyranny on me, without intent, I'll grant you, but can't you see, it's tyranny nevertheless. Your jealousy, your random moods brought on by your bloody depression, and your insecurities. I know you can't help it. I know you can't change, but all the same…"

'Island!' I repeated.

'And you know what? Just like in the old days, it manifests itself whenever you decide you can tell me what I can or cannot do. And you know what else? Whether I decide to publish this or not is so immaterial, I swear to God, I don't care. In fact I had no intention of doing that anyway. But the fact that you're telling me I won't, that I can't, like it's against some law, that's the thing that really bothers me.

'Island!'

He sighed. 'You're still the same old Olivia. You'll always be the afraid.'

I ran away. You don't know me, Harry. Always the same. I've changed so much. So, what you said cannot be true.

Suddenly I feel the shock of cold water on my toes. The sea. The water has swollen. Not from the past. From the real, from the right now. Lily is out there. How would she know the way back? I feel sick again, not from what I might gain, but from what I might lose.

'Lily!' I call out, 'Lily!'

She does not answer. I wait. Thoughts race. No, God, no.

'Lily!' I scream.

I hear voices, calling, from along the beach, men, children, I hear crying, a sort of mixed crying. I cannot go to them. I dare not go to them. And lose my place. This is where Lily went in. Right here. I can't leave this spot.

Lily! Lily!

I don't know what happened next. I think I must be sobbing. My brain churning. Find her Harry. Please. But Harry is gone. And Lily went in here. I must go after her…so I stand up.

A cold hand touches me. She stands before me all wet, shivering. Lily. I grab her, I smother her with all of me, wrap my coat and my skin against hers. I kiss her so hard it must hurt the both of us.

Where did you go? Why didn't you call back when I called out? She pushes me away. There's anger in my voice. She shakes her head.

'It doesn't matter. Not right now. Come on Olivia. It's better you see for yourself. You'll never believe it. Come look' she says. 'Just. Come look.'

What? What?

I follow like a child lost then found. She leads me across the pebbles, I hold her hand for dear life. I see figures in the gloom. Looming larger. Several of them. None of it making sense.

'What…?'

My feet slip, I stumble, on something.

'Look,' I said. Lily keeps going. I look down.

It's something orange. Large, orange, plasticky. Then I see another, and another, and another. Life jackets. Big. Small. It's flotsam….and jetsam. What was it that Harry said? When does one become the other? But this is different. This is people.

Nancy's Video

Maria called. Nancy had been admitted overnight. Her tumour had grown some more. The cancer that had taken over her liver, gotten into her lungs, obliterated her left arm and shoulder, was now hitting her right and left hip, and commenced a journey down her legs. Only God knew how my sister was still breathing.

I drove from Kidderminster in the middle of the night, and arrived too early. I parked outside Costa Coffee on the Mayflower estate, a retail park. It was 6 and Costa opened at 7. I tried to have a nap but workers were arriving in their cars and I'm a poor sleeper. I was the first customer at the door when the café opened.

After that it was surreal. Going to Nancy's house. Entering the hallway. Maria, her daughter, and carer, had left the lights on in the hallway and living room. Everything looked tidy and looked after. Except for the bananas on the dining table, which were turning brown. Milk in the fridge was a bit whiffy. Poppy, Nancy's poodle, had gone home with Maria. Poppy's water bowl was full. Nancy's life was on show everywhere. Her and her five kids mostly smiling contentedly from various moments in their lives, gazing back at me from photos hanging in every room. Happier times. I could feel my cheeks burning, my stomach tightening, and my eyes holding back the tears.

I managed a shower, then drove to the hospital. It was a painful journey. Traffic was congested. I joined a long, angry queue for the multi-storey.

When I reached Kingswood Ward, a visitor's sign said 11.30 onwards. I had an hour to kill. I bought a paper at the hospital shop, went to the restaurant, and slumped in a seat for a while. The restaurant was busy, mostly filled with permutations of visiting families, absorbed in their own dramas. I kept one eye on the time.

Nancy laid on her back, the upper sheet of her bed kicked away. She wore a light cotton nightdress with some delicate pastel floral design. Somehow the skin of her face, legs and lower torso, had spread like soft dough, merging with the mattress, as though she was sinking into the bed. I kissed my sister.

She smiled. A beautiful smile despite half her teeth being missing.

"Hello brother," her voice was muted.

"So, how are you?" It's a stupid question, but you really want to know.

"I'm okay now. They gave me morphine."

Nancy was diagnosed 18 years ago. About her illness, she never complained. Just gave you facts.

"So out of 10, how much pain?"

She gave it some thought.

"I would say, between 9 and a half, and ten."

"So, if I can imagine that level of pain, it's the kind where you'd like someone to shoot you and…"

"Yep. Yesterday. If someone had given me a gun I would have done it then," she said, half smiling.

There was a small commotion down the hall. Doctors' rounds commenced. Nurses went into action. Blue screens were drawn all around. The nurses disappeared. Dr Wu, a short grey-haired man wearing a dark blue apron, came into view. A young Indian woman in a similar outfit followed on his heels. She remained standing, a serious face behind large spectacles, holding tightly onto a clipboard. Dr Wu was thin faced with kind brown eyes. He sat down and drew his chair close to Nancy, on the opposite side of the bed. I stretched forward to hear him. Mostly his questions related to how she was feeling.

"Whatever you need", he said at the conclusion. "It's about finding the right amount of medication for you. There's no limit on the morphine. If you need to go to the bathroom, you can ask for some Oromorph, if you want to get up and walk about, have some more Oromorph."

"Is there any news from Guy's?" she asked.

"No, but we are hoping we might hear something today."

"What about the radiotherapy? Am I going to be moved?"

"Again. We are still waiting for the oncologist's report, hopefully that will come today too," he said.

My sister thanked him. We both did. Doctors get thanked a lot even when nothing happens.

Over the next few hours, the daughters arrived separately. First Maria, then Betty, the eldest, later Olivia, the youngest, which made the full complement of daughters. Of the two sons, Ben was at work, Jake, the eldest, was on holiday in Dubai. Each arrival sparked hugs and greetings. Nancy welcomed them all. Thankfully, the morphine was kicking in, freeing her to reassure the kids with some self-deprecating jokes and painless laughter. We traded glances, with a mutual feeling that everything might be all right after all.

*

Later, it was just Nancy, Maria and me. Two MacMillan nurses showed up. Julie, tall and blonde, Jackie, short and dark. Both in their twenties, both pretty. Julie, the blonde, sat where Dr Wu had been, and began talking. She sort of followed Dr Wu's script at first, but included the word palliative three times in the first two minutes. It was the first time the words had been uttered during Nancy's care. The words hit me like large stones. I watched them pass over my sister's head, she was smiling away, she and Julie were getting on like new best pals, but I saw Maria almost lose her balance at the end of the bed, and had to turn her face away.

"Is there a chance we can get Nancy home?" I said.

"Every chance," said Julie. "We need to assess the amount of medication that's right for Nancy first, and how she would manage on only four visits per day."

"I'll move in when mum gets discharged," said Maria.

"That'd be a great help," said Julie.

"What about the chemotherapy?" Maria asked. "She has the medication for it in her drawer but it's not been given to her yet."

"I don't want it Maria," said Nancy. "I've had enough. Besides, what good does it do?"

No one had an answer to that.

The next day I was in my car, about to drive to the hospital, when Betty called.

"Uncle, have you heard Maria's message on Whatsapp?"

"No. Not yet. Why?"

"I'm upset. I'm really worried she's trying to take over. Promise me you won't let that happen."

"I'm sorry Betty, I don't understand."

Betty started crying.

"She said mum's coming off the chemotherapy tablets..., I was with her..., at Guy's last week..., and she definitely said she wanted to have the treatment. She's had them for three days and she's been alright up till now. I just don't understand **why** she's not been given them at the hospital."

"I don't know why either Betty. But I'm pretty sure your mum doesn't want them anymore. But I promise you, if it helps, I will check again with her."

"If you don't mind." Betty began to sob loudly. "I'm finding this really difficult."

"I know."

"I thought I was stronger than I am."

"You are strong," I said.

"I'm not." (sniff) "I'm really not."

Nancy was sat upright in a chair next to the bed when I reached her. There was a rosy colour in her cheeks, her hair had been combed tidily. She wore a dark blue T shirt with the words 'Hello Weekend' embroidered in white cotton. There was a word search book on the table in front of her, she removed her spectacles for me.

"Hello brother," she said, again with the smile.

"You look great," I said, handing her a salted caramel latte. I meant it too.

"Oh, thank you."

"We need to talk sis. Before anyone else gets here."

"Oh. Okay."

I sat down beside her.

"What you said about the chemotherapy yesterday. About not wanting to go on with it. Are you sticking to that?"

Nancy looked me straight in the eye.

"Yes," she said firmly.

"Ok. Do you remember all those years ago when we did that Power of Attorney for you, and you decided on Ben and Maria being the names that went on the form?"

"I do."

"And not too long ago, when Betty found out she wasn't on the list, she freaked out, and when she challenged you, you said it was me who did the form?"

Nancy bit her lip.

"Nancy, there's confusion happening now, about your medication this time. And if we don't stop it, I can see major arguments developing between your kids. Lasting resentments. Do you mind if we talk about what you really want to do? And why. And sis, this time, I really need you to own your decision."

Nancy explained how she felt, and why. I called a male nurse. We found a box of Pazopanib tablets in the drawer next to her bed. He confirmed these were the chemotherapy tablets. I went through the list of side effects with Nancy. Diarrhoea? She nodded. Skin problems? She showed me her arms, the upper areas of her skin were covered in bloody smears. Headaches, loss of appetite, lost sense of taste, bloating, nausea. She had them all. I knew this was a rehearsal. I asked her if she would repeat what she had just told me on my phone, by way of a video recorded message. She agreed.

The Video

Nancy: Tell my kids, that I love every one of them, from my kids, to my grandchildren, and my great grandchild. I also said, that when I do go, I do not want to be buried. I only want a cremation.

I'd like my ashes to be scattered with Tisha's (her previous dog)

Me: Okay. Let's just talk about the medication now. You have choices to make, and I want them to be your decisions. Only yours. So, with respect to chemotherapy, what's your view on that?

Nancy: My chemotherapy, it makes me feel ill. I hurt everywhere. I get really tired. Also, my taste buds are going. I can't really eat anything. This is why, I end up losing a lot of weight, through that. I don't really want to keep taking tablets, I'm sick of them. Really, really sick of them. So, I just don't want to keep doing that. All I want to do is, when the time comes, (her voice starts to break up here), just to go. I just want to go, and that's it. I know people will be hurt. When I'm gone. I don't want them to be moping. I don't want them crying. I know they will sometimes. But I do not want them spending their times, thinking about…and

Maria, (Nancy laughs) find a nice rich bloke and go and get married and live in Greece. Whatever you want.

Later, I call her children, my nephews and nieces, one by one. As I speak to them, I remind myself they are no longer kids. They've grown, experienced life, marriage, had their own kids. But I do believe that when the umbilical cord is severed, an invisible one remains, and the invisible one is even more painful when cut; call it a feeling, spiritual if you like. I know the knife is out, and explain what has been discussed, why it has been discussed, and that there is a video I could send if they wanted. To my great surprise, all of them ask to have a copy.

Later I get calls, thanking me for the video. The clarity it provides. Ben text me to say it will help him with the grieving process. I am still unsure. But it is done, and for now it feels like the right thing. The last few days have been exhausting. The journey home seems endless. The M25 motorway has seized up, a lorry has crashed up ahead. Two hours have dragged by and nothing has moved. A few of us leave our cars to walk up and down the tarmac, talking to other drivers. My phone rings. It's Maria.

"Uncle," she says, "You're an executor of mum's will."

"Yes Maria."

"Well, I know it says the house to be divided into five equal parts, but I want dad to get some of the money too."

I had gone over Nancy's will last month. No mention of Maria's father, her ex, as a recipient. I have a feeling of foreboding, that Maria's wish spells trouble.

"Ok," I say. "I'm listening."

(For my sister, who passed away in July 2024)

Yellow

Once upon a time, and for rather a long time, there was a man named Harry. One morning, Harry noticed he was turning yellow so he went to Northumberland House to see a doctor. It wasn't good news.

On his way home, Harry had a lot to think about. He took a detour through Park Lane cemetery and went to speak to his dead wife. He often did this when he had a load to get off his chest. He told her everything that had been done, and what the doctor had said. She listened patiently, wisely refraining from offering advice. After their spiritual conversation he decided two things. First, to ditch his mobile phone. Second, to read all the books he'd stacked up over the years—books he had never found the time to read.

Hm. There must be two to three hundred books in all. I'd better crack on. I'll see you, my love.

While walking through the cemetery towards an exit, Harry tossed his phone in a bin, immediately feeling a sense of relief. He looked over his shoulder to check his dead wife wasn't trailing him. It was curious habit she had when she was alive, and something she persisted in well after she had gone. Sometimes he got a glimpse of her, a few steps back. Sometimes she would follow him all the way home just to make sure he got back safe. Then she would head back to the cemetery, job done. This time, the coast was clear.

Good, he thought, *I must be doing the right thing.*

The house was modest—a narrow, two-up, two-down—Victorian in style, charming but showing a few signs of neglect. The wrinkles of which were only evident with closer inspection.

When he entered the house he headed straight for the upstairs spare bedroom, directly for where he had a mini-library, which he had affectionately named *Minnie*. Minnie was a short and wide bookcase, made up of four rows of shelves—nothing distinguishing, except for the fact that she had carried so many books for so many years she had begun to look as tired as the house. In fact, some of the shelves were beginning to splinter, which made it precarious to draw out a book on occasion.

Harry swiped a finger across one of them, to his great shame it came away with a thick dry coating of dust.

"Oh dear," he said, more to himself than to Minnie or the books.

During his senior years, Harry had developed a habit of talking to inanimate objects around the house. His wife had noticed this months before she died, but kept quiet on the matter. Except to say, sometimes she felt a twinge of jealousy when she felt Harry should be sharing his feeling more with her. She confided that to Harry just one time. Harry carried on regardless. He had come to believe that, by developing a little rapport, objects that might otherwise be awkward if they chose to be, often responded in a very positive way. For example, locks, can openers, bottle caps, tv remotes—each seemed to have a wilfulness, a distinct voice, a personality if you like. After his wife had gone, Harry began to make the time to listen.

With one exception that is, that of the room housing Minnie, his mini library, a room he had largely ignored of late. So when he opened the door, he was ready for a cold reception, which is exactly what he got.

"What do you want?" barked Minnie in her raspy voice.

Harry winced. "Oh dear lord, I've neglected you, haven't I? Poor old thing."

"Neglected? Excommunicated more like. Jolly good thing I've got the spiders for company," Minnie quipped. "If not for them, I'd be completely potty by now. No thanks to you, mate."

This was a slap in the face. Harry knew it was deserved.

He took a moment to survey the room. Facing the spiders was his least favourite part of Minnie's upkeep. Over in one corner were a couple of large hairy ones, near to the window. If they were a couple, he couldn't tell. They remained perfectly still, as spiders often do when someone enters their space. They were clearly waiting for a reaction from Harry to how they had been marking their territory. It had been a long time since Harry had tended to the room.

"I'm sorry Minnie, really," he said. "But things have changed, and I promise—for as long as I live, never to forget you again."

"Oh?" remarked Minnie, sceptically. "You sure about that? I mean, what is the point of having a bookshelf and all these bloody books if you aren't going to use them?"

"I can't really argue with you," he said.

"Then tell me, why should I believe that things are going to change?"

"Oh Yes. Because they will. In fact, they already have. Dramatically. I was coming to tell you anyway. I've come up with a plan to read all the books I've never touched, which means you're going to see a lot more of me from now on. I won't stop until I'm done either. What do you say to that?"

Minnie let out a short whistle, not easy for a bookshelf, which was why she then fell quiet, as though contemplating his proposition.

Harry twiddled his thumbs while the contemplating took place.

Finally, Minnie said. "You feeling alright? You're looking a bit yellow—about as yellow as the pages of *Lord Jim* on the second shelf."

Harry spotted the book, looking very sorry for itself. He chuckled. "*Lord Jim* is as yellow as an autumn leaf."

"Ain't that the truth," Minnie echoed.

"I'll admit," Harry said with a sigh. "I'm not feeling great. Truth is, I don't think I'll ever feel great again."

Minnie's voice softened at hearing this. "Well then, if you'll excuse the pun, I guess we have a mini deal. But just one thing... You did say 'promise.' To me, that's such a big word. So if you are serious about such and undertaking, I'm telling you you'd better keep it, and also be quick about it. I mean look at me. I'm not sure how much longer I can hold these buggers up, especially that blooming thesaurus."

Harry nodded, removed the Thesaurus as a show of good will, which happened to be the largest book on the shelf. As a further sweetener, he assured Minnie that every finished book would go straight to a charity shop, so she wouldn't have to carry them ever again.

Kicking off with a pot of Darjeeling tea, Harry and Minnie then discussed a strategy for tackling the collection which they agreed to call "the great unread." Harry figured he'd start with his favourites—modern classics, including Japanese authors like Murakami and Yagisawa, masters of fantasy and illusion. Didn't it make sense to start with the books you enjoyed the most?

After that the British authors—Greene, Le Carré, Boyd—past masters of intrigue, deception, and betrayal. These writers made up the bulk of his collection. Follow up, perhaps some Europeans—Keun, Saint-Exupéry, Ferranti, Calvinin, Bassoni.

Minnie, sounded more enthused now, suggested following up with the Scandinavian authors, whose introspective, melancholic tales of isolation and suicide had always intrigued Harry.

"Health permitting," Harry said, "If I can then I'll tackle the great American novels after that—Baldwin, Davis, the depictions of injustice and survival through history. I do regret not finishing Hemingway and Chandler in my younger days."

"And the poets?" Minnie asked, sounding a bit wary.

"Ah, the poets... what do you reckon? Maybe save them until last? Latin, Greek—perhaps I'll skip them altogether."

"No offence," Minnie said calmly, "but do you think you will live long enough to make it to the classics?"

Harry grinned. "Can you imagine my poor, departed body found with *Paradise Lost* or *The Iliad* in my hand? I wouldn't want that."

"Me neither," Minnie chuckled. "So, where do we start?"

Harry spotted a *Kawakami, Strange Weather in Tokyo.*

"I know exactly," he said, grinning.

The Gift

Over the following months, Harry read aloud to Minnie. First, he set up a chair beside her, a small table with space for a book and a cup of tea. He also added a small turntable so they could listen to music, mainly classical piano works by Schubert and Rachmaninov. Over time, Harry added a standard lamp, setting it next to Minnie and the small table, explaining how this would allow them to read late into the night. Then an electric kettle and a teapot came along, which he placed in the remaining corner away from the spiders, which started to look ever larger, probably due to the biscuit crumbs Harry didn't bother sweeping up. Sometimes Harry would fall asleep in his chair rather than seek his own bed, after a time wake up refreshed, brew up another cup of tea, and continue where he left off. He was starting to get used to the spiders by now. No longer afraid they might 'do something' while he was asleep. The spiders were also encouraged by the fact there webs by and large were left alone. To boot, it seemed as though they were transfixed while he was there, like they were listening too, which is ridiculous, but who really knows? Over time they gradually began to draw nearer, both intrigued and comforted by the new sounds and light, and biscuit crumbs.

Harry read with enunciation, even on his worst days. He'd stop occasionally to consult Minnie, asking for her take on things. A library contains a lot of knowledge, after all.

Then something remarkable happened. Minnie began to develop a consciousness. Of course, it may have just been the fact that Harry might be growing more senile, but what did that matter? It was just the two of them, and how would he know the difference?

"I think I am beginning to have a consciousness," she told him. "You don't mind, do you?"

Harry was a little sceptical. After all, she was just a manifestation of his own thought. But he didn't tell her that.

"On the contrary," he said. "I am delighted. It is like a gift."

How wonderful to bounce ideas off each other, rather than just fire words at an inanimate object.

The new development wasn't perfect. It needed time to manifest.

At first, Minne was slow to respond to the back-and-forth, slow to contribute with her own intellectual exchange of views. But after a while, Minnie realized she was far more worldly than she had originally thought, and she began to challenge Harry's thinking, with words like...

"I think this is what Orwell meant when he said…"

Even when Harry was in a lot of pain she was not deterred from her argument.

"No, no, no Harry! You're barking up the wrong tree here!"

Of course, Harry was very pleased to be put on the right path.

It was a far stranger sensation for Minnie, especially considering she had spent her life as an inanimate object. Books had always been her raison d'être, but it was more about their weight and size than content, but now, somehow, as a real game changer, she could absorb their content. A real turning point came when Harry told her she was created from what was once a living thing. This sparked off Minnie's newborn imagination, and as we know, with a young imagination, anything seems possible.

"I wasn't surprised when you told me about how things were progressing in your mind," Harry said one day, "it makes sense—because you're made of paper, paper comes from trees, and books come from paper. It may be hard to believe. We're kind of one blood, at least of similar DNA."

It was food for thought at least.

When autumn came. The house stood mainly in the dark. A lot of the time it rained outside. Harry was thinner than Minnie could remember. His bouts of sleep grew longer in tandem with the nights. And their conversations shorter.

Out of affection, Minnie waited patiently for Harry to wake up.

"Hi Minnie. Must have dropped off there. You ok?" he asked.

"I have a question for you? One I can't really answer myself."

"Do you? Well then. Fire away!"

"Am I still alive? I mean, am I organic?"

"Well now. That is a question. Erm. Erm. Not being no scientist. I don't really know the answer to that," Harry said, "Organically, probably not alive, but in the quantum world, you're made of tiny particles, and those particles are always in motion. So yes, I would say on one level you are alive, just in a different way."

"So, in that sense, we're the same?" Minnie asked, a note of wonder, and hope, contained in her voice.

"Yes," Harry said simply, unable to theorise further.

From this point forward, their conversations orbited around life and death, prompted by the books they read, but also by Harry's failing health. They wandered through Satre's mind as regards existentialism. Freud and Yalom's on psychology. Harry threw in Bertrand Russell as it had been a great help to him in life. As their collected knowledge of varied philosophies about existence grew, Minnie's mind expanded in ways she had never imagined possible.

"Harry," she asked one day, "I know it may sound a bit obsessive, but I'd really like to know where I come from. For example. What kind of tree was I made from? Was I part of a forest? Did I overlook the sea? Am I native or foreign? Could I have come from some faraway land? Do you think you could help? I don't know who else to ask?"

Harry considered her pleas for information. He felt an acute sadness. Was it any different to an adopted child coming to an age where they demanded some answers from their fake parents, about their origin? He didn't think so.

"Please, Harry, if you could only help me understand this. It would be the greatest gift you could give to me."

To his credit, despite growing yellower by the day, much darker now than the copy of the Lord Jim novel, Harry agreed he would do his best to get some answers.

Bone

PC Markham had never been to a sudden death before, but as everyone bar the station cleaner had told him, it was part and parcel of the job. As soon as he entered the dilapidated house, he already knew what to expect—that he would find an 80-year-old man, and he would be lifeless. There were piles of unopened mail by the front door, colonies of flies at every window—many already dead. This told him everything he needed to know.

"It's the smell that gets you," his Sergeant had warned over a mug of tea.

He didn't want to proceed further, on account that the smell had invaded his system already.

"It smells here," he said aloud.

A neighbour had called the police, concerned after not seeing Harry Green for months. The front garden had grown wild, wilder than was usual, and Harry Green's bushes had ignored any sort of protocol and were beginning to invade the neighbouring yard. The neighbour had tried to help, but stressed to Pc Markham when he arrived, that it wasn't his job to tend to Mr. Green's garden.

After a cursory look through the downstairs rooms, PC Markham steeled himself to head upstairs. Floorboards creaked beneath his feet, and the buzzing of flies grew more intense as he approached, as if anticipating he was there to set them free. Finally, Pc Markham stood at the threshold of an open door.

You just know, he thought to himself.

Inside, the room was still, the air thick with the smell of decay. He wanted to gag and run out. Instead, he fought of the impulse, pulled out a hanky, and used it to pinch his nose as he entered.

Oh dear lord, he thought as soon as he saw what he saw.

Later, in his report, he would note that Mr. Green's body was shrouded in cobwebs. His skin bloated, and darkened, with pockets of air trapped beneath. Flies had feasted around Harry Green's face, leaving the bones of his forehead and nose exposed. Yet, despite the grotesque scene, there was something also serene about it. No signs of a struggle, no indication of foul play.

On the floor near Mr. Green's outstretched hand lay a copy of *Oscar Wilde's Complete Works*. The officer recalled something about Wilde from school, something his teacher used to repeat. "Now Wilde, he would say, one of the greats in literature, now he was a funny man."

Spiders had spun webs traversing the space between Mr. Green's body and a nearby bookcase, which seemed somewhat unnecessary. Everything connected by gossamer. The bookcase was almost empty, carrying about twenty books, and one shelf was missing entirely. PC Markham thought it odd at first, then found it leaning against a wall, standing upright in a bowl. *That is even odder*, he told himself.

A local GP arrived to certify death. She confirmed Mr. Green had likely passed away weeks earlier, although she couldn't pinpoint an exact date.

"He ignored every attempt to reach him," the GP explained, her face soft with regret. "He refused treatment, wouldn't even return our calls. I'm afraid he gave up."

"What about family?" asked the officer.

"According to records, there's no one left. He survived everyone."

As the doctor examined the scene, PC Markham noticed something strange. A small, bright green shoot was emerging from the base of the bookshelf. The lower end of the bookshelf had been placed in a bowl, but if there had been water there it had now dried up completely. But that new sprout, it was rooted in the wood itself.

He called the doctor over.

"That's impossible, isn't it?" he observed, "But you tell me... it seems alive."

"What's that?" said the doctor, distractedly.

"Come and take a look for yourself."

The doctor stepped forward, puzzled.

"Hm. I've seen stranger things, but honestly, nothing like that, but I'm not really a biologist, so…"

She went back to her examination, making some notes on a form.

Pc Markham examined the shelf more closely, just to make sure he wasn't seeing things. No. No. The little plant seemed to be defying logic—but there it was, growing in the strangest of places.

"What, say, if reason can be put to one side for a moment, life has found a way to bloom in the most unexpected corner of the world?"

The doctor looked at him like he was crazy. "You sure you want to put that in your report? You are a newbie after all."

Pc Markham said nothing and waited until after the doctor had gone, then transported the shelf into the back garden and rested it under an apple tree.

That should give it a chance, he thought.

The doctor was right, of course, none of this extra information was included in his final report. That would only lead to unnecessary complications. It would go down as a natural death after all.

Later that day, when Pc Markham was back home, sat in front of the TV with his girlfriend with a packet of crisps, he made a mention of it to see what his girlfriend's take of it might be. But she was more interested in watching First Dates, and a few minutes later he forgot about it.

Jack and Kate

When Jack arrived at Kate's home, his heart sank. It was Tuesday, and Mr Hilliard's car was still on the drive. Usually, Kate's father would have set out for work. The 1-year-old Ford Fiesta sat proudly afront the five-bedroom house, on a crazy paved sloping drive, nose pointing to the road. It was shiny and fresh as though made ready to leave a showroom. The turquoise blue paintwork gleamed in the morning sun. The front passenger seats had not yet breathed the air beyond the plastic covers which had been there from day one. Jack thought carefully about where to place his bike.

He hauled it up the drive away to the right, weighed a foot on the kick stand, propped it up, then regarded it for a moment. It bore scars and dents from when he had recently come off.

After checking its stability, he removed his crash helmet, exposing his skin to the brisk spring morning. Sweat around his face and neck turned cold.

He was 3 years older than Kate, who was 19. They had been courting for a year. Kate's home was on a main road on the furthest edge of east London. The house in comparison to Jack's, was 'posh'. Jack lived on a council estate, in a house with draughty aluminium window frames and damp walls. On top of that there was the rent, which they could barely afford. Everything about Kate's was originally beyond what he knew and had taken time to get used to. Now it was familiar. He unzipped his green parka coat, took a deep breath, then knocked.

The rap sparked a flurry of movement from behind the door, two then three pastel colours, yellow, lilac and green, milled about the hallway and the kitchen. Kate's voice first. Then Rebecca's. Rather, Rebecca's protests, 'definitely complaining' about something. Rebecca had her own way of expressing her dissatisfaction with an idea, expecting little quarter, then withdrawing to her room. The eldest child at 23, she had developed an individual sense of dress, comprising a variety of purple outfits. If it wasn't purple then it wasn't part of her wardrobe. Jack spotted her purple figure as it bolted up the stairs. The larger yellow figure disappeared into the kitchen.

Kate opened the door, a few inches shorter than him, and looked up.

Right away he could see she had been crying. The tears had taken nothing away. Her face was beautifully round, punctuated with dark brown eyes that could melt him without trying, her high cheekbones caressed by wavy chestnut hair which fell to her shoulders. On any other day he would be thinking of how to play with her hair.

Those brown eyes were now probing his, and Jack, being rubbish at eye contact, pulled her towards him and kissed her. Gently, lingeringly.

Needing to feel she was kissing him back. And she was. And the thought crossed his mind, they might still be ok.

"Mum's in there," she said. "Go say hello."

He left his helmet on the floor of the hallway, and followed her towards the kitchen. Kate let him go in first. Marianne was there, in a long yellow dress, her weight resting on the edge of the kitchen sink, seemingly transfixed by the sight of the rear garden. She was short and wide, with fleshy hands, a hearty laugh, and a big heart. I didn't take long for Jack to work out that she was the glue that held everything in the Hilliard household together, she was the cook, the cleaner, the carer, the key decision maker, the one everyone looked to, indeed needed, to take responsibility in a crisis. Marianne had raised three children, the middle one, Kevin, was currently studying art at Oxford university, the eldest stayed home on account of her autism, and the youngest, Kate, worked in London as an insurance clerk. Mr Hilliard, Marianne's husband, was a quiet and diminutive figure in comparison. He was the provider, and had risen through the office ranks of a large corporation to senior management level, but rarely liked to socialise, even at home, and rarely appeared except for meals or to watch a tv show he liked.

Jack crossed the kitchen floor. Marianne was facing but not looking at the garden. Her head was lowered. Her eyes fixed on a bowl of dirty crockery inside the sink.

He placed a hand on her shoulder.

"Hi Marianne," he said.

"Oh Jack," she replied, shaking her head. "This is all very sad. Whichever way one looks at things, it's so sad."

"I know," said Jack. "And I am sorry."

Just then, heavy footsteps rumbled over their heads. Jack wondered if it might be intentional. Most likely. Mr Hilliard had a right to be angry. He was expressing himself in footsteps. They sure sounded like some kind of statement.

Marianne reached for Jack's hand, pulled it towards her and pressed a bunch of keys into his palm. "He says you're to take Kate in the car."

There was more banging about overhead. They both looked up.

"He doesn't want to see you, he's not ready, if you can understand…, but Kate can't drive, not today, and I, I mean we, expect it'll be safer than your bike, especially now you've learned to drive."

"OK," said Jack." I'll make sure we get there…I promise to take it slow."

She nodded.

"Thank you Jack. He said if you leave now, you'll have plenty of time to find a parking space. Hackney can get quite busy at this time of day."

They hugged before he left.

***

The way the doors whumped shut, the car became a vacuum. In the sudden quiet, Kate asked him if he had the money.

The money. Jack felt the weight of it against his chest on his way up, and at last was relieved to remove it from his jacket pocket.

"It's all here," he said, passing her an envelope. Kate tucked the envelope into her handbag and shut it tight. He took a moment to look at her.

She had decided on a light blue raincoat. Below that a white blouse beneath a green cardi, and a knee length skirt. Black high heeled shoes. These were her office clothes.

He turned the ignition key. For a while after that, they spoke only when it was necessary for directions. This was Kate's neighbourhood, so Jack did as he was told, mindful of Marianne's request, he decided to stay at least five miles an hour below the varied speed limits along the way, nervously slowing way ahead of upcoming junctions, unwilling to chance an amber light. He couldn't speak to her. It was like his tongue had become stuck to the roof of his mouth.

Eventually, along the main road towards Hackney, they joined a queue of traffic. It barely crawled along.

Jack checked his watch. The engine quietly idled. Jack had an urge to switch on the car radio, but resisted it. Instead, he looked at Kate. She looked sad, but beautiful.

"Are you sure this is what you want?" she asked quietly.

"You know I don't. I don't think want is the right word. But we agreed about this. We both said it was right. Didn't we? For now anyway."

"Why?"

"What?"

"Say why again. I need to hear you say it. I need to know again."

"But. We've talked about this, Kate, haven't we? So many times."

She produced a tissue and wiped her nose with it.

"I'm sorry, I know. Can't you see, I have to ask. It's like my head's mixed up Jack. First I think I know, then I know I don't. I forget why we are doing this, you can understand that can't you? I think this is what you want more than me."

Jack knew. What Kate had said was true. He could turn around and she would be delighted. An unwanted resentment seared through him every time she said it. He hated himself. For what this journey was leading to. He didn't want to think about it, talk about it. He didn't ever ask a burning question. But he thought it anyway. And his eyes had given him away. Had this been deliberate? She said no. It just happened. He never asked when. He just knew. A November night. Too cold to journey back on the bike. He stayed over. For some reason, the bed in Keith's room had been moved to the opposite side of the house, to make room for lots of suitcases and storage boxes, and the bed was now up against a window facing the main road. There were no curtains for some reason. The room was lit by moonlight. He waited for her, his pulse racing. As per usual, when all the house lights went off, he heard Kate's light footsteps approaching. She appeared like a ghost at the door, he followed the movements of the ghost as it glided towards his embrace. The moon, fiercely bright in all its radiance, took full view of them, coating their skin with ivory. Everything about Kate was irresistible. Her lips, her hair. His blood burned for her. He would never forget the feeling of not being in control of anything, the wave of impossible desire that took over, the feeling of letting go. As though being directed by a wild force of nature. Nature knows better than me, he thought. Leave yourself in nature's hands. He did.

When he regained himself, the moon had reduced to being the ordinary moon it was before, and under its light, Kate was sobbing uncontrollably.

In front of them, cars shuffled forwards at a snail's pace.

"I don't have a job, I don't have anywhere we can live. We can't live at mum's. She would hate you. I don't want her to hate you Kate."

"She hates me already, so what difference does it make?"

"No. She doesn't."

"You just can't see it. My mum said, if necessary, we could live at mine."

"Really? Your dad hates me, he thinks I'm a waster. He doesn't see all the applications I've had rejected. Months and months of them. I'm really struggling just to get an interview, and then when I do, I'm either overqualified or have no experience. That's all I get. And what if I don't get a job, what then? What will you think of me, when I can't support, us?"

"He doesn't think that. At least he won't, once you find work."

"Exactly. I would think the same in his shoes. I think that about myself now."

"We're here," she said. "It's that building on the left. Look. You can go in that space there.

***

It resembled a temporary council office, one of those demountable things they'd started building at secondary schools and infant schools that had no money, maybe this one was a bit bigger. The exterior walls were light grey and there was a flat felted roof. A single step led to a double door. There was an intercom to one side. The paintwork on the timber windows was cracking. You couldn't see inside. There were net curtains everywhere. There was a signboard in front, a large white board on two stilts, saying Family Planning Clinic, with an arrow below the words pointing to reception.

Kate told him to remain in the car. She had already been here twice before to discuss what would happen.

"I don't want you in there," she said.

"*Ok,*" he said.

While sat in the car, Jack scanned the car park. The overall shape was square, coated in black tarmac, large enough for about ten to twelve vehicles, six on either side of the square. Alongside, two cars down, there was a man, very tanned, much older than him, sat in the driver's seat of a red BMW. The man stared at him. Nodded in his direction. Their eyes connected for a moment, enough to reach some sort of understanding, enough to realise that the man was expecting something, maybe a sign, back from Jack. Jack only felt revulsion and looked away, not daring to look back.

***

Kate sobbed quietly most of the way back, like she was crying inside herself, a pain that was not for sharing, but she couldn't hold on to it all. Jack felt numb.

"Are you in pain?" he asked.

"No. They gave me something."

"Oh. OK."

They were close to Kate's house now. She sighed.

"When we get back. You can't stay. Not today."

"Ok. Can I come over at the weekend? Not to stay. Just to see you. We could go to a movie. If you felt like it."

"Maybe. I don't know."

"I'm sorry Kate. I don't think I can say it enough."

"No. You can't. You knew what this meant to me."

He pulled the car up on the drive. His bike was still standing where he left it.

He switched the engine off. It creaked a bit. The sun had gone in.

“I saw it, she said. Then she started crying.

He held her tightly, for a while, while she buried her head in his neck. Then she pushed him away and got out of the car. He watched her disappear inside without looking back. Marianne came out with his crash helmet. They hugged and said farewell, it felt like a last farewell. Jack grabbed his gloves from the topbox. Kate’s helmet was there too, and his Post Office Savings book. Red. Passport looking. One corner of it clipped.

Marianne waved him off.

It wasn’t until he got around the corner and out of view, when he started to cry.

On and off after that. All the way home.

The Kidderminster Coffee Club (pt 1)

Men need to talk to other men. They need to laugh, but they also need to talk.

Not exactly a revelation but I had never really thought about it much, not at all before the football accident. My quadricep got torn away from my kneecap and floated around my thigh like a giant lump of mozzarella. The solution was urgent surgery, a hole in the knee and the loose end of the muscle sewn in. This I received five days before moving the 160 miles to Kidderminster. I was told to wear a splint for 16 weeks, even while in bed. I remember excruciating pain, and never feeling so helpless in all my life.

Moving to Kidderminster meant that two of my three brothers-in-law now lived nearby. Sympathetic to my plight, and looming despondency, they responded marvellously. Both Fat Pep, so called for his resemblance to Pep Guardiola, and Four Tops, for his constantly feeling the cold for most of the year, were well versed on my deep addiction to morning coffee. They turned up at my door, almost daily, to taxi the 'southern' patient to a local cafe. They carefully escorted me plus crutches from house to the back seat of their respective cars, where I could lie the whole width of the car with my right leg fully stretched, my back propped up against a rear door, then drive me to the Costa Coffee café in Crossley Park. It required effort and care, and a degree of tenderness I did not know they had until then.

To my further surprise, Four Tops, who declared he never liked coffee his whole life, began to knock back cortados, a short milky coffee fortified with two shots of coffee grounds. Most people would start at least with a latte or a cappuccino. In car terms, that was like going from 0 – 60 in about 10 seconds. Fat Pep loved the new arrangement because he could socialise in the mornings as well now.

Over the weeks, our group of three grew into many more. Spontaneous bursts of laughter emanating from our corner table drew both approval and disapproval in varying amounts, but mostly positive.

On two occasions, women approached our table on their way out, stopping to express how nice it was to hear men laugh. Their comments struck me. The inference was these ladies did not often hear men laugh. Could this be right?

Our corner became a human snowball if you like, men only, growing larger by the week just through talking and laughing, sometimes so hard it hurt. Reuben and son. Then James. Four Tops' mate Brensly, recently retired. Brensly introduced Nick the Fireman, both Nick and Brensly knew Radar so it seemed reasonable he should come along too. After that, Mick the Geordie, Will the priest. Big John and Tik Tok. A Greek Cypriot called Giorgos who ran a fine chip shop.

Tables got dragged together to form a single long one. Not every day. Mondays and Fridays mainly.

Fat Pep and myself were retired police officers. Fat Pep's new life was training Wim Hof therapy at a local arboretum, teaching students to breathe more deeply, offering the experience of using ice cold water to suppress inflammation. Fat Pep sported an official shirt to promote his courses. That is how we met Tik Tok, who came over to ask about Fat Pep's shirt. Tik Tok had once served in the Royal Navy and been assigned to working on the Royal Yacht. He knew most of the Royal Family, Princess Di, the Queen. He does not really need a description; he has a loud voice which cannot be set to 'low.'

What a motley lot we were. What diverse skills we had. Or had, though I am pretty sure these skills never die, rather they rust. A detective, a police trainer, a Dunlop tyres engineer, furniture cum car salesman, IT manager, car light designer, mechanical engineer/manager of a large big firm, a fireman turned trainer of army personnel, a builder/fighter/security man who can take on pretty much anything, a restaurant manager. Ages between 50 up to 70, which means ailments like gout, high blood pressure, dicky hearts, tricky bladders, and forgetfulness are factors on how and if we can get to the table or not. Happily, these medical predicaments are rarely the subject of conversation.

One cold, dark, and wet September Friday, the majority of us were sat around our elongated table, waiting for the arrival of Tik Tok. It was 'cake Friday' and Tik Tok buys the cakes. True to form he is tardy. The eyes of my companions' dart between their drinks and the car park, scanning for Tik Tok's large black van.

Seated to my left is Fat Pep, late 50s, a large man with a shiny head to match his hearty demeanour and radiant smile. To my right is Four Tops. Overtly far more serious than his brother, a bit Italian looking, a master of irony. Four Tops has peppery long hair, quite long and deep lines beneath his eyes which contribute to his Italian-ness. Four Tops is as ever, armed with sweets, in case Brenly's insulin level plummets. Beside Brensly, was Radar, a nickname he inherited on account of his resemblance to a character in the seventies TV series called MASH. Radar tends to lean back and rest his hands on his portly midriff. He is an easy going, affable fellow, content to go along with the latest car talk but more likely to light up when the subject turns to motorbikes, about which he has his own website. For work, Radar runs projects involving the design of lights for new cars.

So that leaves me. RA Zantis. A 'once was' detective, the guy who gets a headache when he doesn't get his cortado in. My hair has turned white and I hobble from a football injury. I carry a book for when the attendance numbers come to one. A rarity but it happens.

We are the 'once were' group. Once a police officer, once a car salesman, once an IT guy, and so on. Some of us lament the loss of a former profession. I do not, but I do recognise that filling that gap is not always easy.

I am talking to George.

"Zantis," he tells me seriously, "My cod is line caught. You understand?"

He looks for reassurance.

"Yes, I know. You said."

The main topic of conversation is a forthcoming curry night. There is usually one in the pipeline. If not then it is a Comedy night. Intermingled I hear about a forthcoming car show. I can feel myself glazing over.

"Who's in?" says Fat Pep, the main driver for making events happen.

He conducts a round robin, of 'Ayes and Nays, followed by reasons for the Nays.' Excuses are interrupted by a booming voice.

"Bonjour!"

Tik Tok rarely arrives with stealth. His on-deck voice is as audible as a man up in a crow's nest warning 'ship ahoy.' We reciprocate with a quick bonjour, then orders are taken. *A cherry Bakewell if you don't mind...a chocolate brownie, today...no, no, just a croissant today please.*

Tik Tok stares at me enquiringly, his cheeks red full of blood.

"Comment allez vous?" I say.

Tik Tok aims to learn French so he can impress his girlfriend. To assist his aspirations, each time he walks in I greet him this way, and without fail he looks momentarily puzzled, takes a few seconds to search out an appropriate response, then lights up.

"Je suis…tres bien!"

We laugh. Both satisfied. Better some French than none, I think. Lesson over.

"A cake?" he offers.

"No thank you," I say, fully aware that in a while, regardless of my response, a quarter of his cherry Bakewell, plus the whole of the cherry glace, will slide from his side of the table to mine. He goes off to get the cakes in. Tik Tok has a big heart, a childish nature, a generosity that makes me smile.

Conversations become splintered when the goodies arrive.

Four Tops turns to me.

"So did you find out what happened to that guy…er."

"You mean Alan, the one who used to come in on a bike?"

"That's the one."

"Yeah. He lost both legs. He's awaiting prosthetics."

"Er what's that?" Brensly chips in.

I go over the story. Is it a story? A few months ago, one morning at the start of summer, two of the barista women stood at the serving counter, Laurel and Ellen, looked deeply upset.

"What is it?" I asked.

Laurel was trying to shield her face by wiping a hand over her cheeks.

"Alan's thrown himself in front of a train," they say in unison.

I take a while to digest this. Up till then, Alan had been a regular customer. A morning coffee guy. He would sit in the same long sofa, a few yards away, almost parking himself across it like a sleepy cat, and be immersed in a book.

I was touched that Laurel and Ellen were so affected by the fate of a customer.

"He stood up for us one day when a rude man decided to have a go at us." said Laurel. This was new to me. The Alan I knew was mild mannered and softly spoken.

My conversations with him were usually brief, following the same lines.

"Hiya mate." I might say.

He would answer behind a warm smile.

"Hello. How you doing?"

"I'm good thank you. What are you reading now?"

We often held up our books simultaneously. A quick time comparison. Both of us being avid readers, we eventually got round to discussing our favourite novels. To discover we both liked the same authors, was unifying, I think.

Who and what we read inevitably says something about the reader themselves. Our common ground was:

JL Carr, George Orwell, Graham Greene.

Like me, he enjoyed his morning coffee and occasional pauses to people watch.

He would lean his bike outside, against the window. I never saw him with a cycle helmet. Come rain or shine, he wore a straw hat, like a die-hard cricket fan.

One day we were talking.

"Where do you cycle from Alan?"

"Stourport."

"Oh, that far? Along the busy roads?"

"No. I use the canal paths; they lead straight here."

"And you do that, whatever the weather?"

"Yeah. It's no bother."

I tried it once. It is about three miles. I did it with a road bike. The path gets bumpy and narrow on occasion, and once or twice I got stung by overarching nettles, and pricked by an overgrown shrub, but it is still a pleasant way to get from Kidderminster to Stourport; the stillness of the canal, the movement of natural habitat all around, and the safety of being far away from poor drivers.

"You know Alan?" Ellen asked me.

"Yeah. Of course. The reader, comes on a bike."

Amidst her tears, Ellen tells me what she knows. He was hit by a train but did not die. He was going to survive, and live without his legs.

"I'm hoping to visit him in Worcester General Hospital," she said.

I offer to come too.

"That might be too much. Do you mind if we give it time?" she replied.

"No. You're right. But if I can dig up a couple of books before you go see him, would you mind getting them to him?"

She agreed to do this. I carefully considered which books Alan might like to read while restricted to a hospital bed and no doubt in a lot of pain. In the end I decided on a rare JL Carr (A Season in Sinji) and a copy of Keep the Aspidistra Flying by George Orwell.

I presented them to Ellen a few days later.

"I tried calling him," I explain. "He doesn't pick up, or reply to my texts."

"He is too embarrassed," she replies.

"It is a miracle don't you think? How one can throw themselves in front of a train and get that outcome?"

She shrugs her shoulders. I know this might sound cold. Some might say: *It is what it is.* But my nosiness gets in the way. I am a retired detective since 2012, and it still bugs me when I do not have answers to the how and the why.

After recounting all of this to my morning friends on a cake Friday, I still feel bothered.

"It's hard to imagine," says Four Tops, "What goes through someone's mind to go and do something like that."

“Well now, that is a question, isn’t it,” I replied. “Have you ever thought about suicide?”

When I learned about Alan’s terrible injury, I did consider he might tell me so I could write about it, but that was looking increasingly unlikely. Actually, impossible.

Have you ever thought about it?

It is a question not to be directed at anyone, so I threw it open to all the men.

“Nah,” says Four Tops without hesitation. Brensly shakes his head emphatically.

“What about you Pep?”

Fat Pep took a deep breath to allow time to reflect first.

“I never thought about, doing myself in. But when I was going through all the nasty stuff with Annabel, I remember going to bed and wishing I’d never wake up.”

“What about you Tik Tok?”

Tik Tok looked me straight in the eye. And it is there, in his eyes. A story.

“Yeah…

Yeah…

…I have.”

He gives a skeletal outline. Hanging. He got close, but changed his mind at the last second. Best not to examine further. Not there and then.

*

Some days I walk a mile and a half to reach the café. The route takes me down Comberton Hill, a busy main road, past Kidderminster Railway Station. The station has a small border garden which is well tended by volunteers. It was early May when out of the blue, a shrine appeared on the edge of the railway garden. It was impossible not to notice. Everything had been prepared so lovingly. Letters spelling LOUISA were laid out at the very front, afore a short lump of stone, and a plaque which read, 'We walk in the dark, to serve in the light.' Behind the stone was a mass of fresh flowers, four toy windmills spread evenly, and numerous bird feathers, stuck in the grass all around them. A photo frame with four photos inside. A young woman. Mostly my eye was drawn to a row of books placed in front of the flowers, sat upright, just like they would be if placed correctly on a bookshelf. Among them are:

The Astronomy Handbook
Homer: The Odyssey
The Mums Book
A Medical Dictionary
An Italian Dictionary

I thought to myself, *this is no ordinary woman. This woman had a real appetite and zest for life. These books suggest not only a desire to better understand our world, but one to make it better.* It was discombobulating. Why these books have not helped to save her. Just in the same way Alan's books had not prevented him from leaping in front of a train.

The papers do not say the woman, in her early 40s, had fallen deliberately, but there was a line included beneath the article that said:

Whatever you're going through, Samaritans are there – day or night, 365 days a year. You can call them for free on 116 123, e-mail them at jo@samaritans.org, or visit samaritans.org to find your nearest branch.

I had a ton of own books at home. They offer places I can escape to, experiences and ideas where I can temporarily inhabit other people's minds. Perhaps I put too much stock in their power.

*

Yesterday it was just me and Tik Tok in Costa at our usual table. He gave me a knowing look.

"Do you mind?" I said.

"No. I don't."

"And you don't mind if I write about it either?"

"No. You can write what you want."

"So. How did you - go about it?"

"I tried to hang myself in the garage."

"What did you do?"

"I tied a bit of wire around my neck, dropped the remaining length of wire down to my foot and tied it so I could push out with my foot and tighten the wire up here until I passed out."

"Do you mind if we go in to detail?"

"No."

"What type of wire?"

"Electrical. Cable. You know. From a hoover."

"You cut the cable off a vacuum cleaner?"

"Yep. Sat down on the floor and put it round my neck."

"Why?"

"My wife left me, for another man. I didn't know but she had been seeing him for a while. I didn't know anything. I came downstairs early one morning and found her sleeping on the sofa. I said, "What are you doing down here?" She said, "I've had enough. I'm leaving you. She went to her mum's. Took our son. I'm there on me own. Next thing I know, I get a letter, she wants the house. I'm thinking. I got nothing. What's the point?"

"How much planning was involved?"

"None. I came home after a drink with my mates. Even then I didn't know. I remember going in. It was dark. The house felt empty. I thought. Right. I'm gonna do it."

"Just like that?"

"Just like that."

"Did you stop to think, I'm leaving a young boy fatherless?"

"No. Never entered my head. Not once."

"Some people say suicide is a selfish act, people don't think about anyone else and what they go through. What do you think?"

"It is a selfish act. It is. But you're not really thinking that at the time."

"Had you played around with other ways of killing yourself? Like throwing yourself in front of a train, or taking tablets?"

"No. I just thought. If I do it this way, I'll pass out before anything happens. I wouldn't know the rest."

"I know it sounds daft. What were you wearing at the time."

He takes time to think about this.

"I had a shirt on like this…"

"A polo neck?"

"Yeah. With a name across it in white letters. Started with an H."

We go through the brands we know and arrive at Hackett.

"Colour?"

"Blue. Er. Diesel jeans, and socks."

"White socks?"

"No. Oh. I remember now. I didn't sit down in the garage, I went in the house, sat down by the fire, crying, and did it there."

"Did it matter to you how you would be found?"

"No."

"Nor how you would look when you were found?"

"No."

"What stopped you?"

"The phone. I had the wire around my neck, and it rang."

"Your landline?"

"No. My mobile. My wife's name came up. I thought she might be calling to tell me she was coming back, so I answered it. But she wasn't calling me for that. She was moaning down the phone about something else and I thought, you know what. This ain't worth it. She ain't worth it, and in the end, I thought, our marriage wasn't a happy one, I'd been fooling myself, why was I trying to kill myself for an unhappy marriage?"

"You'd been in some kind of denial?"

"About the state of our marriage? Yes."

I told Tik Tok about the shrine on Comberton Hill. Not long ago I had written a story about a man who discovered he had a terminal illness and decided he would dedicate the remainder of his life reading books stacked up on his bookshelf, that had until then not been read. He ends up talking to his bookshelf and believing it talks back. They have many discussions, one of them about which book it was best to be found dead with when the time came. Ultimately, he was very happy to end his days like this.

"I thought books had more power to keep us alive," I said. "But seeing that shrine makes me realise I may be wrong about that."

Tik Tok looked at me intently. With Tik Tok, I feel I can say anything. In the past he has said stupid things. On this occasion it is me who sounds ridiculous – and I can see he knows it too. And in a few seconds, we get to the point where the only thing we can do is laugh.

Acknowledgements

My thanks go out to the following people, for their guidance and support, and not minding too much about me bending their ear from time to time.

To family and close friends who made significant contributions to these stories, and in some cases are still living with the consequences of what happened to them and others. I am grateful for their honesty, patience and understanding.

To Alex Coutts Fender, and Subba Rao, both of whom I met on an Arvon writing course in Hebden Bridge, way back when, and have remained friends with ever since.

To the bell ringers and other good people of St Leonards Church in Clent, but a special thanks to the Bell Captain Martin Whittaker for his advice and patience.

To Anna Webb, Eileen Neal, and Rob Williamson, and Chris Smith, forever members of our self-founded **Writers Therapy Group**.

To Sheila, Libby, Barbara, Margaret and Mary, all current members of the **Stourport Writing Group**, Stourport Library, whose looks were usually more instructive than their kind words.